Woodrow Wilson

Mere Literature and Other Essays

Woodrow Wilson

Mere Literature and Other Essays

ISBN/EAN: 9783743441941

Manufactured in Europe, USA, Canada, Australia, Japa

Cover: Foto ©Andreas Hilbeck / pixelio.de

Manufactured and distributed by brebook publishing software (www.brebook.com)

Woodrow Wilson

Mere Literature and Other Essays

CONTENTS.

*** All but one of the essays brought together in this volume have already been printed, either in the *Atlantic Monthly*, the *Century Magazine*, or the *Forum*. The essay on Burke appears here for the first time in print.

MERE LITERATURE.

I.

"MERE LITERATURE."

A SINGULAR phrase this, "mere literature,"—
the irreverent invention of a scientific age. Literature we know, but "mere" literature? We are
not to read it as if it meant *sheer* literature, literature in the essence, stripped of all accidental or
ephemeral elements, and left with nothing but its
immortal charm and power. "Mere literature" is
a serious sneer, conceived in all honesty by the
scientific mind, which despises things that do not
fall within the categories of demonstrable knowledge. It means *nothing but literature*, as who
should say, "mere talk," "mere fabrication,"
"mere pastime." The scientist, with his head
comfortably and excusably full of knowable things,
takes nothing seriously and with his hat off, except
human knowledge. The creations of the human
spirit are, from his point of view, incalculable
vagaries, irresponsible phenomena, to be regarded

only as play, and, for the mind's good, only as
recreation, — to be used to while away the tedium
of a railway journey, or to amuse a period of rest
or convalescence; mere byplay, mere make-believe.

And so very whimsical things sometimes happen,
because of this scientific and positivist spirit of the
age, when the study of the literature of any language is made part of the curriculum of our colleges. The more delicate and subtle purposes of
the study are put quite out of countenance, and
literature is commanded to assume the phrases and
the methods of science. It would be very painful
if it should turn out that schools and universities
were agencies of Philistinism; but there are some
things which should prepare us for such a discovery. Our present plans for teaching everybody
involve certain unpleasant things quite inevitably.
It is obvious that you cannot have universal education without restricting your teaching to such things
as can be universally understood. It is plain that
you cannot impart "university methods" to thousands, or create "investigators" by the score,
unless you confine your university education to
matters which dull men can investigate, your lab-
oratory training to tasks which mere plodding dili-
gence and submissive patience can compass. Yet,
if you do so limit and constrain what you teach,

you thrust taste and insight and delicacy of perception out of the schools, exalt the obvious and
the merely useful above the things which are only
imaginatively or spiritually conceived, make education an affair of tasting and handling and smelling,
and so create Philistia, that country in which they
speak of " mere literature." I suppose that in
Nirvana one would speak in like wise of " mere
life."

The fear, at any rate, that such things may happen cannot fail to set us anxiously pondering certain questions about the systematic teaching of
literature in our schools and colleges. How are we
to impart classical writings to the children of the
general public? " Beshrew the general public ! "
cries Mr. Birrell. " What in the name of the
Bodleian has the general public got to do with
literature?" Unfortunately, it has a great deal to
do with it; for are we not complacently forcing the
general public into our universities, and are we not
arranging that all its sons shall be instructed how
they may themselves master and teach our literature? You have nowadays, it is believed, only to
heed the suggestions of pedagogics in order to know
how to impart Burke or Browning, Dryden or Swift.
There are certain practical difficulties, indeed ; but
there are ways of overcoming them. You must

have strength if you would handle with real mastery the firm fibre of these men; you must have a heart, moreover, to feel their warmth, an eye to see what they see, an imagination to keep them company, a pulse to experience their delights. But if you have none of these things, you may make shift to do without them. You may count the words they use, instead, note the changes of phrase they make in successive revisions, put their rhythm into a scale of feet, run their allusions — particularly their female allusions — to cover, detect them in their previous reading. Or, if none of these things please you, or you find the big authors difficult or dull, you may drag to light all the minor writers of their time, who are easy to understand. By setting an example in such methods you render great services in certain directions. You make the higher degrees of our universities available for the large number of respectable men who can count, and measure, and search diligently; and that may prove no small matter. You divert attention from thought, which is not always easy to get at, and fix attention upon language, as upon a curious mechanism, which can be perceived with the bodily eye, and which is worthy to be studied for its own sake, quite apart from anything it may mean. You encourage the examination of forms, grammatical and metrical, which can be quite accurately determined and quite exhaustively catalogued. You bring all the visible phenomena of writing to light and into ordered system. You go further, and show how to make careful literal identification of stories somewhere told ill and without art with the same stories told over again by the masters, well and with the trans-figuring effect of genius. You thus broaden the area of science; for you rescue the concrete phenomena of the expression of thought — the necessary syllabification which accompanies it, the inevitable juxtaposition of words, the constant use of particles, the habitual display of roots, the inveterate repetition of names, the recurrent employment of meanings heard or read — from their confusion with the otherwise unclassifiable manifestations of what had hitherto been accepted, without critical examination, under the lump term " literature," simply for the pleasure and spiritual edification to be got from it.

An instructive differentiation ensues. In contrast with the orderly phenomena of speech and writing, which are amenable to scientific processes of examination and classification, and which take rank with the orderly successions of change in nature, we have what, for want of a more exact term, we call " mere literature," — the literature which is not an expression of form, but an expression of spirit. This is a fugitive and troublesome thing, and perhaps does not belong in well-conceived plans of universal instruction; for it offers many embarrassments to pedagogic method. It escapes all scientific categories. It is not pervious to research. It is too wayward to be brought under the discipline of exposition. It is an attribute of so many different substances at one and the same time, that the consistent scientific man must needs put it forth from his company, as without responsible connections. By "mere literature" he means mere evanescent color, wanton trick of phrase, perverse departures from categorical statement, — something *all* personal equation, such stuff as dreams are made of.

We must not all, however, be impatient of this truant child of fancy. When the schools cast her out, she will stand in need of friendly succor, and we must train our spirits for the function. We must be free-hearted in order to make her happy, for she will accept entertainment from no sober, prudent fellow who shall counsel her to mend her ways. She has always made light of hardship, and she has never loved or obeyed any, save those who were of her own mind, — those who were indulgent to her humors, responsive to her ways of

thought, attentive to her whims, content with her
" mere " charms, She already has her small following of devotees, like all charming, capricious
mistresses. There are some still who think that
to know her is better than a liberal education,

There is but one way in which you can take
mere literature as an education, and that is directly,
at first hand. Almost any media except her own
language and touch and tone are non-conducting.
A descriptive catalogue of a collection of paintings
is no substitute for the little areas of color and
form themselves. You do not want to hear about
a beautiful woman, simply, — how she was dressed,
how she bore herself, how the fine color flowed
sweetly here and there upon her cheeks, how her
eyes burned and melted, how her voice thrilled
through the ears of those about her. If you have
ever seen a woman, these things but tantalize and
hurt you, if you cannot see her. You want to be
in her presence. You know that only your own
eyes can give you direct knowledge of her. Nothing but her presence contains her life. 'T is
the same with the authentic products of literature.
You can never get their beauty at second hand, or
feel their power except by direct contact with them.
It is a strange and occult thing how this quality
of " mere literature " enters into one book, and is

absent from another; but no man who has once
felt it can mistake it.   I was reading the other
day a book about Canada.   It is written in what
the reviewers have pronounced to be an " admirable, spirited style."   By this I take them to mean
that it is grammatical, orderly, and full of strong
adjectives.   But these reviewers would have known
more about the style in which it is written if they
had noted what happens on page 84.   There a
quotation from Burke occurs.   ".There is," says
Burke, " but one healing, catholic principle of
toleration which ought to find favor in this house.
It is wanted not only in our colonies, but here. The
thirsty earth of our own country is gasping and
gaping and crying out for that healing shower from
heaven.   The noble lord has told you of the right
of those people by treaty ; but I consider the right
of conquest so little, and the right of human nature
so much, that the former has very little consideration with me.   I look upon the people of Canada
as coming by the dispensation of God under the
British government.   I would have us govern it in
the same manner as the all-wise disposition of
Providence would govern it.   We know he suf-
fers the sun to shine upon the righteous and the
unrighteous ; and we ought to suffer all classes to
enjoy equally the right of worshiping God accord-

ing to the light he has been pleased to give them." The peculiarity of such a passage as that is, that it needs no context. Its beauty seems almost independent of its subject matter. It comes on that eighty-fourth page like a burst of music in the midst of small talk, — a tone of sweet harmony heard amidst a rattle of phrases. The mild noise was unobjectionable enough until the music came. There is a breath and stir of life in those sentences of Burke's which is to be perceived in nothing else in that volume. Your pulses catch a quicker movement from them, and are stronger on their account.

It is so with all essential literature. It has a quality to move you, and you can never mistake it, if you have any blood in you. And it has also a power to instruct you which is as effective as it is subtle, and which no research or systematic method can ever rival. 'T is a sore pity if that power cannot be made available in the classroom. It is not merely that it quickens your thought and fills your imagination with the images that have illuminated the choicer minds of the race. It does indeed exercise the faculties in this wise, bringing them into the best atmosphere, and into the presence of the men of greatest charm and force; but it does a great deal more than that. It acquaints the mind, by direct contact, with the forces which really govern and modify the world from generation to generation. There is more of a nation's politics to be got out of its poetry than out of all its systematic writers upon public affairs and constitutions. Epics are better mirrors of manners than chronicles; dramas oftentimes let you into the secrets of statutes; orations stirred by a deep energy of emotion or resolution, passionate pamphlets that survive their mission because of the direct action of their style along permanent lines of thought, contain more history than parliamentary journals. It is not knowledge that moves the world, but ideals, convictions, the opinions or fancies that have been held or followed; and whoever studies humanity ought to study it alive, practice the vivisection of reading literature, and acquaint himself with something more than anatomies which are no longer in use by spirits.

There are some words of Thibaut, the great jurist, which have long seemed to me singularly penetrative of one of the secrets of the intellectual life. "I told him," he says, — he is speaking of an interview with Niebuhr, — "I told him that I owed my gayety and vigor, in great part, to my love for the classics of all ages, even those outside the domain of jurisprudence." Not only the gayety and vigor of his hale old age, surely, but also his insight into the meaning and purpose of laws and institutions. The jurist who does not love the classics of all ages is like a post-mortem doctor presiding at a birth, a maker of manikins prescribing for a disease of the blood, a student of masks setting up for a connoisseur in smiles and kisses. In narrating history, you are speaking of what was done by men; in discoursing of laws, you are seeking to show what courses of action, and what manner of dealing with one another, men have adopted. You can neither tell the story nor conceive the law till you know how the men you speak of regarded themselves and one another; and I know of no way of learning this but by reading the stories they have told of themselves, the songs they have sung, the heroic adventures they have applauded. I must know what, if anything, they revered; I must hear their sneers and gibes; must learn in what accents they spoke love within the family circle; with what grace they obeyed their superiors in station; how they conceived it politic to live, and wise to die; how they esteemed property, and what they deemed privilege; when they kept holiday, and why; when they were prone to resist oppression, and wherefore, — I must see things with their eyes, before I can comprehend their law books. Their jural re-

lationships are not independent of their way of living, and their way of thinking is the mirror of their
way of living.

It is doubtless due to the scientific spirit of the
age that these plain, these immemorial truths are
in danger of becoming obscured. Science, under
the influence of the conception of evolution, devotes
itself to the study of forms, of specific differences,
of the manner in which the same principle of life
manifests itself variously under the compulsions of
changes of environment. It is thus that it has become " scientific " to set forth the manner in which
man's nature submits to man's circumstances;
scientific to disclose morbid moods, and the conditions which produce them; scientific to regard
man, not as the centre or source of power, but as
subject to power, a register of external forces instead of an originative soul, and character as a
product of man's circumstances rather than a sign
of man's mastery over circumstance. It is thus
that it has become " scientific " to analyze language as itself a commanding element in man's life.
The history of word-roots, their modification under
the influences of changes wrought in the vocal
organs by habit or by climate, the laws of phonetic
change to which they are obedient, and their persistence under all disguises of dialect, as if they

were full of a self-originated life, a self-directed energy of influence, is united with the study of grammatical forms in the construction of scientific conceptions of the evolution and uses of human speech. The impression is created that literature is only the chosen vessel of these forms, disclosing to us their modification in use and structure from age to age. Such vitality as the masterpieces of genius possess comes to seem only a dramatization of the fortunes of words. Great writers construct for the adventures of language their appropriate epics. Or, if it be not the words themselves that are scrutinized, but the style of their use, that style becomes, instead of a fine essence of personality, a matter of cadence merely, or of grammatical and structural relationships. Science is the study of the forces of the world of matter, the adjustments, the apparatus, of the universe; and the scientific study of literature has likewise become a study of apparatus, — of the forms in which men utter thought, and the forces by which those forms have been and still are being modified, rather than of thought itself.

The essences of literature of course remain the same under all forms, and the true study of literature is the study of these essences, — a study, not of forms or of differences, but of likenesses, — like-

nesses of spirit and intent under whatever varieties
of method, running through all forms of speech
like the same music along the chords of various in-
struments.   There is a sense in which literature is
independent of form, just as there is a sense in
which music is independent of its instrument.   It
is my cherished belief that Apollo's pipe contained
as much eloquent music as any modern orchestra.
Some books live ; many die : wherein is the secret
of immortality ?   Not in beauty of form, nor even
in force of passion.   We might say of literature
what Wordsworth said of poetry, the most easily
immortal part of literature : it is " the impassioned
expression which is in the countenance of all science ;
it is the breath of the finer spirit of all knowledge."
Poetry has the easier immortality because it has
the sweeter accent when it speaks, because its
phrases linger in our ears to delight them, because
its truths are also melodies.   Prose has much to
overcome, — its plainness of visage, its less musical
accents, its homelier turns of phrase.   But it also
may contain the immortal essence of truth and
seriousness and high thought.   It too may clothe
conviction with the beauty that must make it shine
forever.   Let a man but have beauty in his heart,
and, believing something with his might, put it
forth arrayed as he sees it, the lights and shadows

falling upon it on his page as they fall upon it in his heart, and he may die assured that that beauty will not pass away out of the world.

Biographers have often been puzzled by the contrast between certain men as they lived and as they wrote. Schopenhauer's case is one of the most singular. A man of turbulent life, suffering himself to be cut to exasperation by the petty worries of his lot, he was nevertheless calm and wise when he wrote, as if the Muse had rebuked him. He wrote at a still elevation, where small and temporary things did not come to disturb him. 'T is a pity that ·for some men this elevation is so far to seek. They lose permanency by not finding it. Could there be a deliberate regimen of life for the author, it is plain enough how he ought to live, not as seeking fame, but as deserving it.

> "Fame, like a wayward girl, will still be coy
> To those who woo her with too slavish knees;
> But makes surrender to some thoughtless boy,
> And dotes the more upon a heart at ease.
>
> . . . .
>
> "Ye love-sick bards, repay her scorn with scorn;
> Ye love-sick artists, madmen that ye are,
> Make your best bow to her and bid adieu;
> Then, if she likes it, she will follow you."

It behooves all minor authors to realize the possibility of their being discovered some day, and exposed to the general scrutiny. They ought to live as if conscious of the risk. They ought to purge their hearts of everything that is not genuine and capable of lasting the world a century, at least, if need be. Mere literature is made of spirit. The difficulties of style are the artist's difficulties with his tools. The spirit that is in the eye, in the pose, in mien or gesture, the painter must find in his color-box; as he must find also the spirit that nature displays upon the face of the fields or in the hidden places of the forest. The writer has less obvious means. Word and spirit do not easily consort. The language which the philologists set out before us with such curious erudition is of very little use as a vehicle for the essences of the human spirit. It is too sophisticated and self-conscious. What you need is, not a critical knowledge of language, but a quick feeling for it. You must recognize the affinities between your spirit and its idioms. You must immerse your phrase in your thought, your thought in your phrase, till each becomes saturated with the other. Then what you produce is as necessarily fit for permanency as if it were incarnated spirit.

And you must produce in color, with the touch of imagination which lifts what you write away from the dull levels of mere exposition. Black-

and-white sketches may serve some purposes of the artist, but very little of actual nature is in mere black-and-white. The imagination never works thus with satisfaction. Nothing is ever conceived completely when conceived so grayly, without suffusion of real light. The mind creates, as great Nature does, in colors, with deep chiaroscuro and burning lights. This is true not only of poetry and essentially imaginative writing, but also of the writing which seeks nothing more than to penetrate the meaning of actual affairs, — the writing of the greatest historians and philosophers, the utterances of orators and of the great masters of political exposition. Their narratives, their analyses, their appeals, their conceptions of principle, are all dipped deep in the colors of the life they expound. Their minds respond only to realities, their eyes see only actual circumstance. Their sentences quiver and are quick with visions of human affairs, — how minds are bent or governed, how action is shaped or thwarted. The great " constructive " minds, as we call them, are of this sort. They " construct " by seeing what others have not imagination enough to see. They do not always know more, but they always realize more. Let the singular reconstruction of Roman history and institutions by Theodor Mommsen serve as an illustration. Safe men distrust this great master. They cannot find what he finds in the documents. They will draw you truncated figures of the antique Roman state, and tell you the limbs cannot be found, the features of the face have nowhere been unearthed. They will cite you fragments such as remain, and show you how far these can be pieced together toward the making of a complete description of private life and public function in those first times when the Roman commonwealth was young; but what the missing sentences were they can only weakly conjecture. Their eyes cannot descry those distant days with no other aids than these. Only the greatest are dissatisfied, and go on to paint that ancient life with the materials that will render it lifelike, — the materials of the constructive imagination. They have other sources of information. They see living men in the old documents. Give them but the torso, and they will supply head and limbs, bright and animate as they must have been. If Mommsen does not quite do that, another man, with Mommsen's eye and a touch more of color on his brush, might have done it, — may yet do it.

It is in this way that we get some glimpse of the only relations that scholarship bears to literature. Literature can do without exact scholarship, or any scholarship at all, though it may impoverish itself thereby; but scholarship cannot do without literature. It needs literature to float it, to set it current, to authenticate it to the race, to get it out of closets, and into the brains of men who stir abroad. It will adorn literature, no doubt; literature will be the richer for its presence; but it will not, it cannot, of itself create literature. Rich stuffs from the East do not create a king, nor warlike trappings a conqueror. There is, indeed, a natural antagonism, let it be frankly said, between the standards of scholarship and the standards of literature. Exact scholarship values things in direct proportion as they are verifiable; but literature knows nothing of such tests. The truths which it seeks are the truths of self-expression. It is a thing of convictions, of insights, of what is felt and seen and heard and hoped for. Its meanings lurk behind nature, not in the facts of its phenomena. It speaks of things as the man who utters it saw them, not necessarily as God made them. The personality of the speaker runs throughout all the sentences of real literature. That personality may not be the personality of a poet: it may be only the personality of the penetrative seer. It may not have the atmosphere in which visions are seen, but only that in which men and affairs look keenly cut in outline, boldly massed in bulk, consummately grouped in detail, to the reader as to the writer. Sentences of perfectly clarified wisdom may be literature no less than stanzas of inspired song, or the intense utterances of impassioned feeling. The personality of the sunlight is in the keen lines of light that run along the edges of a sword no less than in the burning splendor of the rose or the radiant kindlings of a woman's eye. You may feel the power of one master of thought playing upon your brain as you may feel that of another playing upon your heart.

Scholarship gets into literature by becoming part of the originating individuality of a master of thought. No man is a master of thought without being also a master of its vehicle and instrument, style, that subtle medium of all its evasive effects of light and shade. Scholarship is material; it is not life. It becomes immortal only when it is worked upon by conviction, by schooled and chastened imagination, by thought that runs alive out of the inner fountains of individual insight and purpose. Colorless, or without suffusion of light from some source of light, it is dead, and will not twice be looked at ; but made part of the life of a great mind, subordinated, absorbed, put forth with authentic stamp of currency on it, minted at some definite mint and bearing some sovereign image, it

will even outlast the time when it shall have ceased
to deserve the acceptance of scholars, — when it
shall, in fact, have become "mere literature."

Scholarship is the realm of nicely adjusted opinion. It is the business of scholars to assess evidence and test conclusions, to discriminate values
and reckon probabilities. Literature is the realm
of conviction and vision. Its points of view are as
various as they are oftentimes unverifiable. It
speaks individual faiths. Its groundwork is not
erudition, but reflection and fancy. Your thoroughgoing scholar dare not reflect. To reflect is to let
himself in on his material; whereas what he wants
is to keep himself apart, and view his materials in
an air that does not color or refract. To reflect is
to throw an atmosphere about what is in your
mind, — an atmosphere which holds all the colors
of your life. Reflection summons all associations,
and they so throng and move that they dominate
the mind's stage at once. The plot is in their
hands. Scholars, therefore, do not reflect; they
label, group kind with kind, set forth in schemes,
expound with dispassionate method. Their minds
are not stages, but museums; nothing is done
there, but very curious and valuable collections are
kept there. If literature use scholarship, it is only
to fill it with fancies or shape it to new standards,
of which of itself it can know nothing.

True, there are books reckoned primarily books of science and of scholarship which have nevertheless won standing as literature; books of science such as Newton wrote, books of scholarship such as Gibbon's. But science was only the vestibule by which such a man as Newton entered the temple of nature, and the art he practiced was not the art of exposition, but the art of divination. He was not only a scientist, but also a seer; and we shall not lose sight of Newton because we value what he was more than what he knew. If we continue Gibbon in his fame, it will be for love of his art, not for worship of his scholarship. We some of us, nowadays, know the period of which he wrote better even than he did; but which one of us shall build so admirable a monument to ourselves, as artists, out of what we know? The scholar finds his immortality in the form he gives to his work. It is a hard saying, but the truth of it is inexorable: be an artist, or prepare for oblivion. You may write a chronicle, but you will not serve yourself thereby. You will only serve some fellow who shall come after you, possessing, what you did not have, an ear for the words you could not hit upon; an eye for the colors you could not see; a hand for the strokes you missed.

Real literature you can always distinguish by its

form, and yet it is not possible to indicate the
form it should have. It is easy to say that it
should have a form suitable to its matter ; but how
suitable ? Suitable to set the matter off, adorn,
embellish it, or suitable simply to bring it directly,
quick and potent, to the apprehension of the reader ?
This is the question of style, about which many
masters have had many opinions ; upon which you
can make up no safe generalization from the practice of those who have unquestionably given to the
matter of their thought immortal form, an accent
or a countenance never to be forgotten. Who shall
say how much of Burke's splendid and impressive
imagery is part and stuff of his thought, or tell
why even that part of Newman's prose which is devoid of ornament, stripped to its shining skin, and
running bare and lithe and athletic to carry its
tidings to men, should promise to enjoy as certain
an immortality ? Why should Lamb go so quaintly
and elaborately to work upon his critical essays,
taking care to perfume every sentence, if possible,
with the fine savor of an old phrase, if the same
business could be as effectively done in the plain
and even cadences of Mr. Matthew Arnold's prose ?
Why should Gibbon be so formal, so stately, so
elaborate, when he had before his eyes the example
of great Tacitus, whose direct, sententious style had

outlived by so many hundred years the very language in which he wrote? In poetry, who shall
measure the varieties of style lavished upon similar
themes? The matter of vital thought is not sep-
arable from the thinker; its forms must suit his
handling as well as fit his conception. Any style
is author's stuff which is suitable to his purpose and
his fancy. He may use rich fabrics with which to
costume his thoughts, or he may use simple stone
from which to sculpture them, and leave them
bare. His only limits are those of art. He may
not indulge a taste for the merely curious or fan-
tastic. The quaint writers have quaint thoughts;
their material is suitable. They do not merely
satisfy themselves as virtuosi, with collections of
odd phrases and obsolete meanings. They needed
twisted words to fit the eccentric patterns of their
thought. The great writer has always dignity, restraint, propriety, adequateness; what time he
loses these qualities he ceases to be great. His
style neither creaks nor breaks under his passion,
but carries the strain with unshaken strength. It
is not trivial or mean, but speaks what small meanings fall in its way with simplicity, as conscious of
their smallness. Its playfulness is within bounds;
its laugh never bursts too boisterously into a
guffaw. A great style always knows what it would

be at, and does the thing appropriately, with the larger sort of taste.

This is the condemnation of tricks of phrase, devices to catch the attention, exaggerations and loud talk to hold it. No writer can afford to strive after effect, if his striving is to be apparent. For just and permanent effect is missed altogether unless it be so completely attained as to seem like some touch of sunlight, perfect, natural, inevitable, wrought without effort and without deliberate purpose to be effective. Mere audacity of attempt can, of course, never win the wished for result; and if the attempt be successful, it is not audacious. What we call audacity in a great writer has no touch of temerity, sauciness, or arrogance in it. It is simply high spirit, a dashing and splendid display of strength. Boldness is ridiculous unless it be impressive, and it can be impressive only when backed by solid forces of character and attainment. Your plebeian hack cannot afford the showy paces; only the full-blooded Arabian has the sinew and proportion to lend them perfect grace and propriety. The art of letters eschews the bizarre as rigidly as does every other fine art. It mixes its colors with brains, and is obedient to great Nature's sane standards of right adjustment in all that it attempts.

You can make no catalogue of these features of great writing; there is no science of literature. Literature in its essence is mere spirit, and you must experience it rather than analyze it too formally. It is the door to n[...] and to ourselves. It opens our hearts to rec[...] he experiences of great men and the concep[...] great races. It awakens us to the signi[...] action and to the singular power of men[...] It airs our souls in the wide atmosph[...] templation. " In these bad days, whe[...] ght more educationally useful to [...]ciple of the common pump than Ke[...] a Grecian Urn," as Mr. Birrell says, we cannot afford to let one single precious sentence of " mere literature " go by us unread or unpraised. If this free people to which we belong is to keep its fine spirit, its perfect temper amidst affairs, its high courage in the face of difficulties, its wise temperateness and wide-eyed hope, it must continue to drink deep and often from the old wells of English undefiled, quaff the keen tonic of its best ideals, keep its blood warm with all the great utterances of exalted purpose and pure principle of which its matchless literature is full. The great spirits of the past must command us in the tasks of the future. Mere literature will keep us pure and keep us strong.

Even though it puzzle or altogether escape scientific method, it may keep our horizon clear for us, and our eyes glad to look bravely forth upon the world.

II.

WHO can help wondering, concerning the modern multitude of books, where all these companions of his reading hours will be buried when they die; which will have monuments erected to them; which escape the envy of time and live? It is pathetic to think of the number that must be forgotten, after having been removed from the good places to make room for their betters.

Much the most pathetic thought about books, however, is that excellence will not save them. Their fates will be as whimsical as those of the humankind which produces them. Knaves find it as easy to get remembered as good men. It is not right living or learning or kind offices, simply and of themselves, but — something else that gives immortality of fame. Be a book never so scholarly, it may die; be it never so witty, or never so full of good feeling and of an honest statement of truth, it may not live.

When once a book has become immortal, we think that we can see why it became so. It contained,

we perceive, a casting of thought which could not
but arrest and retain men's attention; it said some
things once and for all because it gave them their
best expression. Or else it spoke with a grace or
with a fire of imagination, with a sweet cadence
of phrase and a full harmony of tone, which have
made it equally dear to all generations of those
who love the free play of fancy or the incomparable
music of perfected human speech. Or perhaps it
uttered with candor and simplicity some universal
sentiment; perchance pictured something in the
tragedy or the comedy of man's life as it was never
pictured before, and must on that account be read
and read again as not to be superseded. There
must be something special, we judge, either in its
form or in its substance, to account for its unwonted
fame and fortune.

This upon first analysis, taking one book at a
time. A look deeper into the heart of the matter
enables us to catch at least a glimpse of a single
and common source of immortality. The world is
attracted by books as each man is attracted by his
several friends. You recommend that capital fellow So-and-So to the acquaintance of others because
of his discriminating and diverting powers of observation: the very tones and persons — it would
seem the very selves — of every type of man live

again in his mimicries and descriptions. He is the
dramatist of your circle; you can never forget him,
nor can any one else; his circle of acquaintances can
never grow smaller. Could he live on and retain
perennially that wonderful freshness and vivacity
of his, he must become the most famous guest and
favorite of the world. Who that has known a man
quick and shrewd to see dispassionately the inner
history, the reason and the ends, of the combinations
of society, and at the same time eloquent to tell of
them, with a hold on the attention gained by a certain quaint force and sagacity resident in no other
man, can find it difficult to understand why we
still resort to Montesquieu? Possibly there are
circles favored of the gods who have known some
fellow of infinite store of miscellaneous and curious
learning, who has greatly diverted both himself
and his friends by a way peculiar to himself of giving it out upon any and all occasions, item by item,
as if it were all homogeneous and of a piece, and
by his odd skill in making unexpected application
of it to out-of-the-way, unpromising subjects, as if
there were in his view of things mental no such dis-
integrating element as incongruity. Such a circle
would esteem it strange were Burton not beloved
of the world. And so of those, if any there be,
who have known men of simple, calm, transparent

natures, untouched by storm or perplexity, whose talk was full of such serious, placid reflection as seemed to mirror their own reverent hearts, — talk often prosy, but more often touchingly beautiful, because of its nearness to nature and the solemn truth of life. There may be those, also, who have felt the thrill of personal contact with some stormy peasant nature full of strenuous, unsparing speech concerning men and affairs. These have known why a Wordsworth or a Carlyle must be read by all generations of those who love words of first-hand inspiration. In short, in every case of literary immortality originative personality is present. Not origination simply, — that may be mere invention, which in literature has nothing immortal about it; but origination which takes its stamp and character from the originator, which is his spirit given to the world, which is himself outspoken.

Individuality does not consist in the use of the very personal pronoun, *I:* it consists in tone, in method, in attitude, in point of view ; it consists in saying things in such a way that you will yourself be recognized as a force in saying them. Do we not at once know Lamb when he speaks? And even more formal Addison, does not his speech bewray and endear him to us? His personal charm is less distinct, much less fascinating, than that

which goes with what Lamb speaks, but a charm he
has sufficient for immortality. In Steele the matter is more impersonal, more mortal. Some of Dr.
Johnson's essays, you feel, might have been written
by a dictionary. It is impersonal matter that is
dead matter. Are you asked who fathered a certain brilliant, poignant bit of political analysis?
You say, Why, only Bagehot could have written
that. Does a wittily turned verse make you hesitate between laughter at its hit and grave thought
because of its deeper, covert meaning? Do you
not know that only Lowell could do that? Do
you catch a strain of pure Elizabethan music and
doubt whether to attribute it to Shakespeare or to
another? Do you not *know* the authors who still
live?

Now, the noteworthy thing about such individuality is that it will not develop under every star, or
in one place just as well as in another; there is an
atmosphere which kills it, and there is an atmosphere which fosters it. The atmosphere which
kills it is the atmosphere of sophistication, where
cleverness and fashion and knowingness thrive:
cleverness, which is froth, not strong drink; fashion, which is a thing assumed, not a thing of
nature; and knowingness, which is naught.

Of course there are born, now and again, as

tokens of some rare mood of Nature, men of so intense and individual a cast that circumstance and surroundings affect them little more than friction affects an express train. They command their own development without even the consciousness that to command costs strength. These cannot be sophisticated ; for sophistication is subordination to the ways of your world. But these are the very greatest and the very rarest ; and it is not the greatest and the rarest alone who shape the world and its thought. That is done also by the great and the merely extraordinary. There is a rank and file in literature, even in the literature of immortality, and these must go much to school to the people about them.

It is by the number and charm of the individualities which it contains that the literature of any country gains distinction. We turn anywhither to know men. The best way to foster literature, if it may be fostered, is to cultivate the author himself, — a plant of such delicate and precarious growth that special soils are needed to produce it in its full perfection. The conditions which foster individuality are those which foster simplicity, thought and action which are direct, naturalness, spontaneity. What are these conditions ?

In the first place, a certain helpful ignorance.

It is best for the author to be born away from literary centres, or to be excluded from their ruling set if he be born in them. It is best thàt he start out with his thinking, not knowing how much has been thought and said about everything. A certain amount of ignorance will insure his sincerity, will increase his boldness and shelter his genuineness, which is his hope of power. Not ignorance of life, but life may be learned in any neighborhood; — not ignorance of the greater laws which govern human affairs, but they may be learned without a library of historians and commentators, by imaginative sense, by seeing better than by reading; — not ignorance of the infinitudes of human circumstance, but these may be perceived without the intervention of universities; — not ignorance of one's self and of one's neighbor; but innocence of the sophistications of learning, its research without love, its knowledge without inspiration, its method without grace; freedom from its shame at trying to know many things as well as from its pride of trying to know but one thing; ignorance of that faith in small confounding facts which is contempt for large reassuring principles.

Our present problem is not how to clarify our reasonings and perfect our analyses, but how to reënrich and reënergize our literature. That literature is suffering, not from ignorance, but from sophistication and self-consciousness; and it is suffering hardly less from excess of logical method. Ratiocination does not keep us pure, render us earnest, or make us individual and specific forces in the world. Those inestimable results are accomplished by whatever implants principle and conviction, whatever quickens with inspiration, fills with purpose and courage, gives outlook, and makes character. Reasoned thinking does indeed clear the mind's atmospheres and lay open to its view fields of action; but it is loving and believing, sometimes hating and distrusting, often prejudice and passion, always the many things which we call the one thing, character, which create and shape our acting. Life quite overtowers logic. Thinking and erudition alone will not equip for the great tasks and triumphs of life and literature: the persuading of other men's purposes, the entrance into other men's minds to possess them forever. Culture broadens and sweetens literature, but native sentiment and unmarred individuality create it. Not all of mental power lies in the processes of thinking. There is power also in passion, in personality, in simple, native, uncritical conviction, in unschooled feeling. The power of science, of system, is executive, not stimulative. I

do not find that I derive inspiration, but only information, from the learned historians and analysts
of liberty; but from the sonneteers, the poets, who,
speak its spirit and its exalted purpose, — who,
recking nothing of the historical method, obey only
the high method of their own hearts, — what may
a man not gain of courage and confidence in the
right way of politics?

It is your direct, unhesitating, intent, headlong
man, who has his sources in the mountains, who
digs deep channels for himself in the soil of his
times and expands into the mighty river, to become
a landmark forever; and not your " broad " man,
sprung from the schools, who spreads his shallow,
extended waters over the wide surfaces of learning,
to leave rich deposits, it may be, for other men's
crops to grow in, but to be himself dried up by a
few score summer noons. The man thrown early
upon his own resources, and already become a conqueror of success before being thrown with the
literary talkers; the man grown to giant's stature
in some rural library, and become exercised there
in a giant's prerogatives before ever he has been
laughingly told, to his heart's confusion, of scores
of other giants dead and forgotten long ago; the
man grounded in hope and settled in conviction
ere he has discovered how many hopes time has

seen buried, how many convictions cruelly given the lie direct by fate; the man who has carried his youth into middle age before going into the chill atmosphere of *blasé* sentiment; the quiet, stern man who has cultivated literature on a little oatmeal before thrusting himself upon the great world as a prophet and seer; the man who pronounces new eloquence in the rich dialect in which he was bred; the man come up to the capital from the provinces, — these are the men who people the world's mind with new creations, and give to the sophisticated learned of the next generation new names to conjure with.

If you have a candid and well-informed friend among city lawyers, ask him where the best masters of his profession are bred, — in the city or in the country. He will reply without hesitation, "In the country." You will hardly need to have him state the reason. The country lawyer has been obliged to study all parts of the law alike, and he has known no reason why he should not do so. He has not had the chance to make himself a specialist in any one branch of the law, as is the fashion among city practitioners, and he has not coveted the opportunity to do it. There would not have been enough special cases to occupy or remunerate him if he had coveted it. He has dared attempt the task of knowing the whole law, and yet without any sense of daring, but as a matter of course.   In his own little town, in the midst of his own small library of authorities, it has not seemed to him an impossible task to explore all the topics that engage his profession ; the guiding principles, at any rate, of all branches of the great subject were open to him in a few books.   And so it often happens that when he has found his sea legs on the sequestered inlets at home, and ventures, as he sometimes will, upon the great, troublous, and much-frequented waters of city practice in search of more work and larger fees, the country lawyer will once and again confound his city-bred brethren by discovering to them the fact that the law is a many-sided thing of principles, and not altogether a one-sided thing of technical rule and arbitrary precedent.

It would seem to be necessary that the author who is to stand as a distinct and imperative individual among the company of those who express the world's thought should come to a hard crystallization before subjecting himself to the tense strain of cities, the corrosive acids of critical circles. The ability to see for one's self is attainable, not by mixing with crowds and ascertaining how they look at things, but by a certain aloofness and self-containment. The solitariness of some genius is not accidental; it is characteristic and essential. To the constructive imagination there are some immortal feats which are possible only in seclusion. The man must heed first and most of all the suggestions of his own spirit; and the world can be seen from windows overlooking the street better than from the street itself.

Literature grows rich, various, full-voiced largely through the re-discovery of truth, by thinking re-thought, by stories re-told, by songs re-sung. The song of human experience grows richer and richer in its harmonies, and must grow until the full accord and melody are come. If too soon subjected to the tense strain of the city, a man cannot expand; he is beaten out of his natural shape by the incessant impact and press of men and affairs. It will often turn out that the unsophisticated man will display not only more force, but more literary skill even, than the trained *littérateur*. For one thing, he will probably have enjoyed a fresher contact with old literature. He reads not for the sake of a critical acquaintance with this or that author, with no thought of going through all his writings and "working him up," but as he would ride a spirited horse, for love of the life and motion of it.

A general impression seems to have gained cur-

rency that the last of the bullying, omniscient
critics was buried in the grave of Francis Jeffrey;
and it is becoming important to correct the misap-
prehension.   There never was a time when there
was more superior knowledge, more specialist
omniscience, among reviewers than there is to-day;
not pretended superior knowledge, but real.   Jeffrey's was very real of its kind.   For those who
write books, one of the special, inestimable advan-
tages of lacking a too intimate knowledge of the
"world of letters" consists in not knowing all that
is known by those who review books, in ignorance
of the fashions among those who construct canons
of taste.   The modern critic is a leader of fashion.
He carries with him the air of a literary worldliness.   If your book be a novel, your reviewer will
know all previous plots, all former, all possible,
motives and situations.   You cannot write anything absolutely new for him, and why should you
desire to do again what has been done already?
If it be a poem, the reviewer's head already rings
with the whole gamut of the world's metrical music;
he can recognize any simile, recall all turns of
phrase, match every sentiment; why seek to please
him anew with old things?   If it concern itself
with the philosophy of politics, he can and will set
himself to test it by the whole history of its kind

from Plato down to Benjamin Kidd. How can it
but spoil your sincerity to know that your critic
will know everything? Will you not be tempted
of the devil to anticipate his judgment or his pre-
tensions by pretending to know as much as he?

The literature of creation naturally falls into two
kinds : that which interprets nature or human action, and that which interprets self. Both of these
may have the flavor of immortality, but neither
unless it be free from self-consciousness. No man,
therefore, can create after the best manner in either
of these kinds who is an *habitué* of the circles
made so delightful by those interesting men, the
modern *literati*, sophisticated in all the fashions,
ready in all the catches of the knowing literary
world which centres in the city and the university.
He cannot always be simple and straightforward.
He cannot be always and without pretension himself, bound by no other man's canons of taste in
speech or conduct. In the judgment of such circles there is but one thing for you to do if you
would gain distinction : you must " beat the record ; " you must do certain definite literary feats
better than they have yet been done. You are
pitted against the literary " field." You are has-
tened into the paralysis of comparing yourself with
others, and thus away from the health of unhesi-

tating self-expression and directness of first-hand vision.

It would be not a little profitable if we could make correct analysis of the proper relations of learning — learning of the critical, accurate sort — to origination, of learning's place in literature. Although learning is never the real parent of literature, but only sometimes its foster-father, and although the native promptings of soul and sense are its best and freshest sources, there is always the danger that learning will claim, in every court of taste which pretends to jurisdiction, exclusive and preëminent rights as the guardian and preceptor of authors. An effort is constantly being made to create and maintain standards of literary worldliness, if I may coin such a phrase. The thorough man of the world affects to despise natural feeling ; does at any rate actually despise all displays of it. He has an eye always on his world's best-manners, whether native or imported, and is at continual pains to be master of the conventions of society ; he will mortify the natural man as much as need be in order to be in good form. What learned criticism essays to do is to create a similar literary worldliness, to establish fashions and conventions in letters.

I have an odd friend in one of the northern counties of Georgia, — a county set off by itself among the mountains, but early found out by refined people in search of summer refuge from the unhealthful air of the southern coast.   He belongs to an excellent family of no little culture, but he was surprised in the midst of his early schooling by the coming on of the war ; and education given pause in such wise seldom begins again in the schools. He was left, therefore, to " finish " his mind as best he might in the companionship of the books in his uncle's library.   These books were of the old sober sort: histories, volumes of travels, treatises on laws and constitutions, theologies, philosophies more fanciful than the romances encased in neighbor volumes on another shelf.   But they were books which were used to being taken down and read ; they had been daily companions to the rest of the family, and they became familiar companions to my friend's boyhood.   He went to them day after day, because theirs was the only society offered him in the lonely days when uncle and brothers were at the war, and the women were busy about the tasks of the home.   How literally did he make those delightful old volumes his familiars, his cronies ! He never dreamed the while, however, that he was becoming learned ; it never seemed to occur to him that everybody else did not read just as he did, in just such a library.   He found out afterwards, of course, that he had kept much more of such company than had the men with whom he loved to chat at the post-office or around the fire in the village shops, the habitual resorts of all who were socially inclined; but he attributed that to lack of time on their part, or to accident, and has gone on thinking until now that all the books that come within his reach are the natural intimates of man.   And so you shall hear him, in his daily familiar talk with his neighbors, draw upon his singular stores of wise, quaint learning with the quiet colloquial assurance, " They tell me," as if books contained current rumor ; and quote the poets with the easy unaffectedness with which others cite a common maxim of the street !   He has been heard to refer to Dr. Arnold of Rugby as " that school teacher over there in England."

Surely one may treasure the image of this simple, genuine man of learning as the image of a sort of masterpiece of Nature in her own type of erudition, a perfect sample of the kind of learning that might beget the very highest sort of literature ; the literature, namely, of authentic individuality.   It is only under one of two conditions that learning will not dull the edge of individuality : first, if one never suspect that it is creditable and a matter of pride to be learned, and so never become learned for the sake of becoming so ; or, second, if it never suggest to one that investigation is better than reflection. Learned investigation leads to many good things, but one of these is not great literature, because learned investigation commands, as the first condition of its success, the repression of individuality.

His mind is a great comfort to every man who has one ; but a heart is not often to be so conveniently possessed. Hearts frequently give trouble ; they are straightforward and impulsive, and can seldom be induced to be prudent. They must be schooled before they will become insensible ; they must be coached before they can be made to care first and most for themselves : and in all cases the mind must be their schoolmaster and coach. They are irregular forces ; but the mind may be trained to observe all points of circumstance and all motives of occasion.

No doubt it is considerations of this nature that must be taken to explain the fact that our universities are erected entirely for the service of the tractable mind, while the heart's only education must be gotten from association with its neighbor heart, and in the ordinary courses of the world. Life is its only university. Mind is monarch, whose laws claim supremacy in those lands which boast the movements of civilization, and it must command all the instrumentalities of education. At least such is the theory of the constitution of the modern world. It is to be suspected that, as a matter of fact, mind is one of those modern monarchs who reign, but do not govern. That old House of Commons, that popular chamber in which the passions, the prejudices, the inborn, unthinking affections long ago repudiated by mind, have their full representation, controls much the greater part of the actual conduct of affairs. To come out of the figure, reasoned thought is, though perhaps the presiding, not yet the regnant force in the world. In life and in literature it is subordinate. The future may belong to it; but the present and past do not. Faith and virtue do not wear its livery; friendship, loyalty, patriotism, do not derive their motives from it. It does not furnish the material for those masses of habit, of unquestioned tradition, and of treasured belief which are the ballast of every steady ship of state, enabling it to spread its sails safely to the breezes of progress, and even to stand before the storms of revolution. And this is a fact which has its reflection in literature. There is a literature of reasoned thought; but by far the greater part of those writings which we reckon worthy of that great name is the product, not of reasoned thought, but of the imagination and of the spiritual vision of those who see, — writings winged, not with knowledge, but with sympathy, with sentiment, with heartiness. Even the literature of reasoned thought gets its life, not from its logic, but from the spirit, the insight, and the inspiration which are the vehicle of its logic. Thought presides, but sentiment has the executive powers ; the motive functions belong to feeling.

"Many people give many theories of literary composition," says the most natural and stimulating of English critics, "and Dr. Blair, whom we will read, is sometimes said to have exhausted the subject; but, unless he has proved the contrary, we believe that the knack in style is to write like a human being. Some think they must be wise, some elaborate, some concise; Tacitus wrote like a pair of stays; some startle us, as Thomas Carlyle, or a comet, inscribing with his tail. But legibility is given to those who neglect these notions, and are willing to be themselves, to write their own thoughts in their own words, in the simplest words, in the words wherein they were thought. . . . Books are for various purposes, — tracts to teach, almanacs to sell, poetry to make pastry; but this is the rarest sort of a book, — a book to read. As Dr. Johnson

said, ' Sir, a good book is one you can hold in your
hand, and take to the fire.'   Now there are ex-
tremely few books which can, with any propriety,
be so treated.   When a great author, as Grote or
Gibbon, has devoted a whole life of horrid industry
to the composition of a large history, one feels one
ought not to touch it with a mere hand, — it is not
respectful.   The idea of slavery hovers over the
Decline and Fall.   Fancy a stiffly dressed gentleman,
in a stiff chair, slowly writing that stiff compilation
in a stiff hand ; it is enough to stiffen you for life."

It is devoutly to be wished that we might learn to
prepare the best soils for mind, the best associations and companionships, the least possible sophistication.   We are busy enough nowadays finding
out the best ways of fertilizing and stimulating
mind ; but that is not quite the same thing as discovering the best soils for it, and the best atmospheres.   Our culture is, by erroneous preference,
of the reasoning faculty, as if that were all of us.
Is it not the instinctive discontent of readers seeking stimulating contact with authors that has given
us the present almost passionately spoken dissent
from the standards set themselves by the realists in
fiction, dissatisfaction with mere recording or observation ?   And is not realism working out upon
itself the revenge its enemies would fain compass?

Must not all April Hopes exclude from their number the hope of immortality?

The rule for every man is, not to depend on the education which other men prepare for him, — not even to consent to it; but to strive to see things as they are, and to be himself as he is. Defeat lies in self-surrender.

This is a plea for the recogn of other standards than used or not in the universities in the world, for the insertion of "heart", of nature untouched by convention, of individual expressing its own spirit unaffected by imposed standards.

Free the creative man from construction

III.

ONCE and again, it would seem, a man is born into the world belated. Strayed out of a past age, he comes among us like an alien, lives removed and singular, and dies a stranger. There was a touch of this strangeness in Charles Lamb. Much as he was loved and befriended, he was not much understood; for he drew aloof in his studies, affected a " self-pleasing quaintness " in his style, took no pains to hit the taste of his day, wandered at sweet liberty in an age which could scarcely have bred such another. " Hang the age!" he cried. " I will write for antiquity." And he did. He wrote as if it were still Shakespeare's day; made the authors of that spacious time his constant companions and study; and deliberately became himself " the last of the Elizabethans." When a new book came out, he said, he always read an old one.

The case ought, surely, to put us occasionally upon reflecting. May an author not, in some degree, by choosing his literary company, choose also his literary character, and so, when he comes to

write, write himself back to his masters? May he
not, by examining his own tastes and yielding himself obedient to his natural affinities, join what congenial group of writers he will? The question can
be argued very strongly in the affirmative, and
that not alone because of Charles Lamb's case. It
might be said that Lamb was antique only in the
forms of his speech; that he managed very cleverly to hit ʌhe taste of his age in the substance of
what he wrote, for all the phraseology had so strong
a flavor of quaintness and was not at all in the
mode of the day. It would not be easy to prove
that; but it really does not matter. In his tastes,
certainly, Lamb was an old author, not a new one;
a "modern antique," as Hood called him. He
wrote for his own age, of course, because there was
no other age at hand to write for, and the age he
liked best was past and gone; but he wrote what
he fancied the great generations gone by would
have liked, and what, as it has turned out in the
generosity of fortune, subsequent ages have warmly
loved and reverently canonized him for writing; as
if there were a casual taste that belongs to a day and
generation, and also a permanent taste which is
without date, and he had hit the latter.

Great authors are not often men of fashion.
Fashion is always a harness and restraint, whether

it be fashion in dress or fashion in vice or fashion in literary art; and a man who is bound by it is caught and formed in a fleeting mode. The great writers are always innovators; for they are always frank, natural, and downright, and frankness and naturalness always disturb, when they do not wholly break down, the fixed and complacent order of fashion. No genuine man can be deliberately in the fashion, indeed, in what he says, if he have any movement of thought or individuality in him. He remembers what Aristotle says, or if he does not, his own pride and manliness fill him with the thought instead. The very same action that is noble if done for the satisfaction of one's own sense of right or purpose of self-development, said the Stagirite, may, if done to satisfy others, become menial and slavish. "It is the object of any action or study that is all-important," and if the author's chief object be to please he is condemned already. The true spirit of authorship is a spirit of liberty which scorns the slave's trick of imitation. It is a masterful spirit of conquest within the sphere of ideas and of artistic form, — an impulse of empire and origination.

Of course a man may choose, if he will, to be less than a free author. He may become a reporter; for there is such a thing as reporting for books as well as reporting for newspapers, and there have been reporters so amazingly clever that their very aptness and wit constitute them a sort of immortals. You have proof of this in Horace Walpole, at whose hands gossip and compliment receive a sort of apotheosis. Such men hold the secret of a kind of alchemy by which things trivial and temporary may be transmuted into literature. But they are only inspired reporters, after all; and while a man was wishing, he might wish to be more, and climb to better company.

Every man must, of course, whether he will or not, feel the spirit of the age in which he lives and thinks and does his work; and the mere contact will direct and form him more or less. But to wish to serve the spirit of the age at any sacrifice of individual naturalness or conviction, however small, is to harbor the germ of a destroying disease. Every man who writes ought to write for immortality, even though he be of the multitude that die at their graves; and the standards of immortality are of no single age. There are many qualities and causes that give permanency to a book, but universal vogue during the author's lifetime is not one of them. Many authors now immortal have enjoyed the applause of their own generations; many authors now universally admired will, let us hope, pass on to an easy immortality. The praise of your own day is no absolute disqualification; but it may be if it be given for qualities which your friends are the first to admire, for 't is likely they will also be the last. There is a greater thing than the spirit of the age, and that is the spirit of the ages. It is present in your own day; it is even dominant then, with a sort of accumulated power and mastery. If you can strike it, you will strike, as it were, into the upper air of your own time, where the forces are which run from age to age. Lower down, where you breathe, is the more inconstant air of opinion, inhaled, exhaled, from day to day, — the variant currents, the forces that will carry you, not forward, but hither and thither.

We write nowadays a great deal with our eyes circumspectly upon the tastes of our neighbors, but very little with our attention bent upon our own natural, self-speaking thoughts and the very truth of the matter whereof we are discoursing. Now and again, it is true, we are startled to find how the age relishes still an old-fashioned romance, if written with a new-fashioned vigor and directness; how quaint and simple and lovely things, as well as what is altogether modern and analytic and painful, bring our most judicious friends crowding, purses in hand, to the book-stalls; and for a while we are puzzled to see worn-out styles and past modes revived. But we do not let these things seriously disturb our study of prevailing fashions. These books of adventure are not at all, we assure ourselves, in the true spirit of the age, with its realistic knowledge of what men really do think and purpose, and the taste for them must be only for the moment or in jest. We need not let our surprise at occasional flurries and variations in the literary market cloud or discredit our analysis of the real taste of the day, or suffer ourselves to be betrayed into writing romances, however much we might rejoice to be delivered from the drudgery of sociological study, and made free to go afield with our imaginations upon a joyous search for hidden treasure or knightly adventure.

And yet it is quite likely, after all, that the present age is transient. Past ages have been. It is probable that the objects and interests now so near us, looming dominant in all the foreground of our day, will sometime be shifted and lose their place in the perspective. That has happened with the near objects and exaggerated interests of other days, so violently sometimes as to submerge and thrust out of sight whole libraries of books. It will not do to reckon upon the persistence of new things. 'T were best to give them time to make trial of the seasons. The old things of art and taste and thought are the permanent things. We know that they are because they have lasted long enough to grow old; and we deem it safe to assess the spirit of the age by the same test. No age adds a great deal to what it received from the age that went before it; no time gets an air all its own. The same atmosphere holds from age to age; it is only the little movements of the air that are new. In the intervals when the trades do not blow, fleeting cross-winds venture abroad, the which if a man wait for he may lose his voyage.

No man who has anything to say need stop and bethink himself whom he may please or displease in the saying of it. He has but one day to write in, and that is his own. He need not fear that he will too much ignore it. He will address the men he knows when he writes, whether he be conscious of it or not; he may dismiss all fear on that score and use his liberty to the utmost. There are some things that can have no antiquity and must ever be without date, and genuineness and spirit are of their number. A man who has these must ever be " timely," and at the same time fit to last, if he can get his qualities into what he writes. He may freely read, too, what he will that is congenial, and form himself by companionships that are chosen simply because they are to his taste ; that is, if he be genuine and in very truth a man of independent spirit. Lamb would have written "for antiquity" with a vengeance had his taste for the quaint writers of an elder day been an affectation, or the authors he liked men themselves affected and ephemeral. No age this side antiquity would ever have vouchsafed him a glance or a thought. But it was not an affectation, and the men he preferred were as genuine and as spirited as he was. He was simply obeying an affinity and taking cheer after his own kind. A man born into the real patriciate of letters may take his pleasure in what company he will without taint or loss of caste ; may go confidently abroad in the free world of books and choose his comradeships without fear of offense.

More than that, there is no other way in which he can form himself, if he would have his power transcend a single age. He belittles himself who takes from the world no more than he can get from the speech of his own generation. The only advantage of books over speech is that they may hold from generation to generation, and reach, not a small group merely, but a multitude of men ; and a man who writes without being a man of letters is curtailed of his heritage. It is in this world of old and new that he must form himself if he would in the end belong to it and increase its bulk of treasure. If he has conned the new theories of society, but knows nothing of Burke; the new notions about fiction, and has not read his Scott and his Richardson; the new criminology, and wots nothing of the old human nature; the new religions, and has never felt the power and sanctity of the old, it is much the same as if he had read Ibsen and Maeterlinck, and had never opened Shakespeare. How is he to know wholesome air from foul, good company from bad, visions from nightmares? He has framed himself for the great art and handicraft of letters only when he has taken all the human parts of literature as if they were without date, and schooled himself in a catholic sanity of taste and judgment.

Then he may very safely choose what company his own work shall be done in, — in what manner, and under what masters. He cannot choose amiss for himself or for his generation if he choose like a man, without light whim or weak affectation; not like one who chooses a costume, but like one who chooses a character. What is it, let him ask himself, that renders a bit of writing a " piece of literature "? It is reality. A " wood-note wild," sung unpremeditated and out of the heart; a description written as if with an undimmed and seeing eye upon the very object described; an exposition that lays bare the very soul of the matter; a motive truly revealed; anger that is righteous and justly spoken; mirth that has its sources pure; phrases to find the heart of a thing, and a heart seen in things for the phrases to find; an unaffected meaning set out in language that is its own, — such are the realities of literature. Nothing else is of the kin. Phrases used for their own sake; borrowed meanings which the borrower does not truly care for; an affected manner; an acquired style; a hollow reason; words that are not fit; things which do not live when spoken, — these are its falsities, which die in the handling.

The very top breed of what is unreal is begotten by imitation. Imitators succeed sometimes, and flourish, even while a breath may last; but "imitate and be damned" is the inexorable threat and prophecy of fate with regard to the permanent fortunes of literature. That has been notorious this long time past. It is more worth noting, lest some should not have observed it, that there are other and subtler ways of producing what is unreal. There are the mixed kinds of writing, for example. Argument is real if it come

vital from the mind; narrative is real if the thing
told have life and the narrator unaffectedly see it
while he speaks; but to narrate and argue in the
same breath is naught.   Take, for instance, the
familiar example of the early history of Rome.
Make up your mind what was the truth of the
matter, and then, out of the facts as you have disen-
tangled them, construct a firmly touched narrative,
and the thing you create is real, has the confidence
and consistency of life.   But mix the narrative
with critical comment upon other writers and their
variant versions of the tale, show by a nice elabo-
ration of argument the whole conjectural basis of
the story, set your reader the double task of doubt-
ing and accepting, rejecting and constructing, and
at once you have touched the whole matter with
unreality.   The narrative by itself might have had
an objective validity; the argument by itself an
intellectual firmness, sagacity, vigor, that would
have sufficed to make and keep it potent; but
together they confound each other, destroy each
other's atmosphere, make a double miscarriage.
The story is rendered unlikely, and the argument
obscure.   This is the taint which has touched all
our recent historical writing.   The critical discussion and assessment of the sources of information,
which used to be a thing for the private mind of

the writer, now so encroach upon the open text that the story, for the sake of which we would believe the whole thing was undertaken, is oftentimes fain to sink away into the foot-notes. The process has ceased to be either pure exegesis or straightforward narrative, and history has ceased to be literature.

Nor is this our only sort of mixed writing. Our novels have become sociological studies, our poems vehicles of criticism, our sermons political manifestos. We have confounded all processes in a common use, and do not know what we would be at. We can find no better use for Pegasus than to carry our vulgar burdens, no higher key for song than questionings and complainings. Fancy pulls in harness with intellectual doubt; enthusiasm walks apologetically alongside science. We try to make our very dreams engines of social reform. It is a parlous state of things for literature, and it is high time authors should take heed what company they keep. The trouble is, they all want to be "in society," overwhelmed with invitations from the publishers, well known and talked about at the clubs, named every day in the newspapers, photographed for the news-stalls; and it is so hard to distinguish between fashion and form, costume and substance, convention and truth, the things

that show well and the things that last well; so
hard to draw away from the writers that are new
and talked about and note those who are old and
walk apart, to distinguish the tones which are
merely loud from the tones that are genuine, to
get far enough away from the press and the hub-
bub to see and judge the movements of the crowd!

Some will do it. Choice spirits will arise and
make conquest of us, not "in society," but with
what will seem a sort of outlawry. The great
growths of literature spring up in the open, where
the air is free and they can be a law unto themselves. The law of life, here as elsewhere, is the
law of nourishment: with what was the earth
laden, and the atmosphere? Literatures are renewed, as they are originated, by uncontrived impulses of nature, as if the sap moved unbidden in
the mind. Once conceive the matter so, and
Lamb's quaint saying assumes a sort of gentle
majesty. A man should "write for antiquity" as
a tree grows into the ancient air, — this old air
that has moved upon the face of the world ever
since the day of creation, which has set the law of
life to all things, which has nurtured the forests
and won the flowers to their perfection, which has
fed men's lungs with life, sped their craft upon the
seas, borne abroad their songs and their cries,

blown their forges to flame, and buoyed up whatever they have contrived. 'T is a common medium, though a various life; and the figure may serve the author for instruction.

The breeding of authors is no doubt a very occult thing, and no man can set the rules of it; but at least the sort of " ampler ether " in which they are best brought to maturity is known. Writers have liked to speak of the Republic of Letters, as if to mark their freedom and equality; but there is a better phrase, namely, the Community of Letters; for that means intercourse and comradeship and a life in common. Some take up their abode in it as if they had made no search for a place to dwell in, but had come into the freedom of it by blood and birthright. Others buy the freedom with a great price, and seek out all the sights and privileges of the place with an eager thoroughness and curiosity. Still others win their way into it with a certain grace and aptitude, next best to the ease and dignity of being born to the right. But for all it is a bonny place to be. Its comradeships are a liberal education. Some, indeed, even there, live apart; but most run always in the market-place to know what all the rest have said. Some keep special company, while others keep none at all. But all feel the atmosphere and life of the place in their several degrees.

No doubt there are national groups, and Shakespeare is king among the English, as Homer is among the Greeks, and sober Dante among his gay countrymen. But their thoughts all have in common, though speech divide them; and sovereignty does not exclude comradeship or embarrass freedom. No doubt there is many a willful, ungoverned fellow endured there without question, and many a churlish cynic, because he possesses that patent of genuineness or of a wit which strikes for the heart of things, which, without further test, secures citizenship in that free company. What a gift of tongues is there, and of prophecy! What strains of good talk, what counsel of good judgment, what cheer of good tales, what sanctity of silent thought! The sight-seers who pass through from day to day, the press of voluble men at the gates, the affectation of citizenship by mere sojourners, the folly of those who bring new styles or affect old ones, the procession of the generations, disturb the calm of that serene community not a whit. They will entertain a man a whole decade, if he happen to stay so long, though they know all the while he can have no permanent place among them.

'T would be a vast gain to have the laws of that community better known than they are. Even the first principles of its constitution are singularly unfamiliar. It is not a community of writers, but a community of letters. One gets admission, not because he writes, — write he never so cleverly, like a gentleman and a man of wit, — but because he is literate, a true initiate into the secret craft and mystery of letters. What that secret is a man may know, even though he cannot practice or appropriate it. If a man can see the permanent element in things, — the true sources of laughter, the real fountains of tears, the motives that strike along the main lines of conduct, the acts which display the veritable characters of men, the trifles that are significant, the details that make the mass, — if he know these things, and can also choose words with a like knowledge of their power to illuminate and reveal, give color to the eye and passion to the thought, the secret is his, and an entrance to that immortal communion.

It may be that some learn the mystery of that insight without tutors; but most must put themselves under governors and earn their initiation. While a man lives, at any rate, he can keep the company of the masters whose words contain the mystery and open it to those who can see, almost with every accent; and in such company it may at last be revealed to him, — so plainly that he may, if he will, still linger in such comradeship when he is dead.

It would seem that there are two tests which admit to that company, and that they are conclusive. The one is, Are you individual? the other, Are you conversable? "I beg pardon," said a grave wag, coming face to face with a small person of most consequential air, and putting glass to eye in calm scrutiny — "I beg pardon; but are you anybody in particular?" Such is very much the form of initiation into the permanent communion of the realm of letters. Tell them, No, but that you have done much better — you have caught the tone of a great age, studied taste, divined opportunity, courted and won a vast public, been most timely and most famous; and you shall be pained to find them laughing in your face. Tell them you are earnest, sincere, consecrate to a cause, an apostle and reformer, and they will still ask you, "But are you anybody in particular?" They will mean, "Were you your own man in what you thought, and not a puppet? Did you speak with an individual note and distinction that marked you able to think as well as to speak, — to be yourself in thoughts and in words also?" "Very well, then; you are welcome enough."

"That is, if you be also conversable." It is

plain enough what they mean by that, too. They mean, if you have spoken in such speech and spirit as can be understood from age to age, and not in the pet terms and separate spirit of a single day and generation. Can the old authors understand you, that you would associate with them? Will men be able to take your meaning in the differing days to come? Or is it perishable matter of the day that you deal in — little controversies that carry no lasting principle at their heart; experimental theories of life and science, put forth for their novelty and with no test of their worth; pictures in which fashion looms very large, but human nature shows very small; things that please everybody, but instruct no one; mere fancies that are an end in themselves? Be you never so clever an artist in words and in ideas, if they be not the words that wear and mean the same thing, and that a thing intelligible, from age to age, the ideas that shall hold valid and luminous in whatever day or company, you may clamor at the gate till your lungs fail and get never an answer.

For that to what you seek admission is a veritable " community." In it you must be able to be, and to remain, conversable. How are you to test your preparation meanwhile, unless you look to your comradeships now while yet it is time to

learn? Frequent the company in which you may
learn the speech and the manner which are fit to
last. Take to heart the admirable example you
shall see set you there of using speech and manner
to speak your real thought and be genuinely and
simply yourself.

The author should deal with
views which are not only
yours, but would last for all time
I'm is more concerned with the freedom
the end. to stand apart, to be
myself, in a world dominated by
"taste" & "fashion."; the right to commune
& the real & permanent, to converse with
old masters & not imitate & how to
contemporary critical standards.

IV.

A LITERARY POLITICIAN.

"LITERARY politician" is not a label much in vogue, and may need first of all a justification, lest even the man of whom I am about to speak should decline it from his very urn. I do not mean a politician who affects literature; who seems to appreciate the solemn moral purpose of Wordsworth's Happy Warrior, and yet is opposed to ballot reform. Neither do I mean a literary man who affects politics; who earns his victories through the publishers, and his defeats at the hands of the men who control the primaries. I mean the man who has the genius to see deep into affairs, and the discretion to keep out of them, — the man to whom, by reason of knowledge and imagination and sympathetic insight, governments and policies are as open books, but who, instead of trying to put haphazard characters of his own into those books, wisely prefers to read their pages aloud to others. A man this who knows politics, and yet does not handle policies.

There is, no doubt, a very widespread skepticism as to the existence of such a man. Many people would ask you to prove him as well as define him; and that, as they assume, upon a very obvious principle. It is a rule of universal acceptance in theatrical circles that no one can write a good play who has no practical acquaintance with the stage. A knowledge of greenroom possibilities and of stage machinery, it is held, must go before all successful attempts to put either passion or humor into action on the boards, if pit and gallery are to get a sense of reality from the performance. No wonder that Sheridan's plays were effective, for Sheridan was both author and actor; but abundant wonder that simple Goldsmith succeeded with his exquisite " She Stoops to Conquer," — unless we are to suppose that an Irishman of the last century, like the Irishman of this, had some sixth sense which enabled him to understand other people's business better than his own; for poor Goldsmith could not act (even off the stage), and his only connection with the theatre seems to have been his acquaintance with Garrick. Lytton, we know, had Macready constantly at his elbow, to give and enforce suggestions calculated to render plays playable. And in our own day, the authors of what we indulgently call " dramatic literature " find themselves constantly obliged to turn tragedies into comedies, comedies into farces, to satisfy the managers; for managers know the stage, and pretend to know all possible audiences also. The writer for the stage must be playwright first, author second.

Similar principles of criticism are not a little affected by those who play the parts, great and small, on the stage of politics. There is on that stage, too, it is said, a complex machinery of action and scene-shifting, a greenroom tradition and practice as to costume and make-up, as to entry and exit, necessities of concession to footlights and of appeal to the pit, quite as rigorous and quite as proper for study as are the concomitants of that other art which we frankly call acting. This is an idea, indeed, accepted in some quarters outside the political playhouse as well as within it. Mr. Sydney Colvin, for example, declares very rightly that: —

" Men of letters and of thought are habitually too much given to declaiming at their ease against the delinquencies of men of action and affairs. The inevitable friction of practical politics," he argues, " generates heat enough already, and the office of the thinker and critic should be to supply not heat, but light. The difficulties which attend his own unmolested task — the task of seeking after and proclaiming salutary truths — should teach him to make allowance for the far more urgent difficulties which beset the politican; the man obliged, amidst the clash of interests and temptations, to practice from hand to mouth, and at his peril, the most uncertain and at the same time the most indispensable of the experimental arts."

Mr. Colvin is himself of the class of men of letters and of thought; he accordingly puts the case against his class much more mildly than the practical politician would desire to see it put. Practical politicians are wont to regard closeted writers upon politics with a certain condescension, dashed with slight traces of uneasy concern. " Literary men can say strong things of their age," observes Mr. Bagehot, " for no one expects that they will go out and act on them. They are a kind of ticket-of-leave lunatics, from whom no harm is for the moment expected; who seem quiet, but on whose vagaries a practical public must have its eye." I suppose that the really serious, practical man in politics would see nothing of satirical humor in such a description. He would have you note that, although traced with a sharp point of wit, the picture is nevertheless true. He can cite you a score of instances illustrative of the danger of putting faith in the political judgments of those who are not politicians bred in the shrewd and moving world of political management.

The genuine practical politician, such as (even our enemies being the witnesses) we must be acknowledged to produce in great numbers and perfection in this country, reserves his acidest contempt for the literary man who assumes to utter judgments touching public affairs and political institutions. If he be a reading man, as will sometimes happen, he is able to point you, in illustration of what you are to expect in such cases, to the very remarkable essays of the late Mr. Matthew Arnold on parliamentary policy and the Irish question. If he be not a reading man, as sometimes happens, he is able to ask, much to your confusion, " What does a fellow who lives inside a library know about politics, anyhow ? " You have to admit, if you are candid, that most fellows who live in libraries know little enough. You remember Macaulay, and acknowledge that, although he made admirable speeches in Parliament, held high political office, and knew all the considerable public men of his time, he did imagine the creation to have been made in accordance with Whig notions ; did hope to find the judgments of Lord Somers some day answering mankind as standards for all possible times and circumstances. You recall Gibbon, and allow, to your own thought at least, that, had he not remained silent in his seat, a very few of his sentences would probably have sufficed to freeze the House of Commons stiff. The ordinary literary man, even though he be an eminent historian, is ill enough fitted to be a mentor in affairs of government. For, it must be admitted, things are for the most part very simple in books, and in practical life very complex. Not all the bindings of a library inclose the various world of circumstance.

But the practical politician should discriminate. Let him find a man with an imagination which, though it stands aloof, is yet quick to conceive the very things in the thick of which the politician struggles. To that man he should resort for instruction. And that there is occasionally such a man we have proof in Bagehot, the man who first clearly distinguished the facts of the English constitution from its theory.

Walter Bagehot is a name known to not a few of those who have a zest for the juiciest things of literature, for the wit that illuminates and the knowledge that refreshes. But his fame is still singularly disproportioned to his charm; and one feels once and again like publishing him, at least to all spirits of his own kind. It would be a most agreeable good fortune to introduce Bagehot to men who have not read him! To ask your friend to know Bagehot is like inviting him to seek pleasure.

Occasionally, a man is born into the world whose mission it evidently is to clarify the thought of his generation, and to vivify it; to give it speed where it is slow, vision where it is blind, balance where it is out of poise, saving humor where it is dry, — and such a man was Walter Bagehot. When he wrote of history, he made it seem human and probable ; when he wrote of political economy, he made it seem credible, entertaining, — nay, engaging even ; when he wrote criticism, he wrote sense. You have in him a man who can jest to your instruction, who will beguile you into being informed beyond your wont and wise beyond your birthright. Full of manly, straightforward meaning, earnest to find the facts that guide and strengthen conduct, a lover of good men and seers, full of knowledge and a consuming desire for it, he is yet genial withal, with the geniality of a man of wit, and alive in every fibre of him, with a life he can communicate to you. One is constrained to agree, almost, with the verdict of a witty countryman of his, who happily still lives to cheer us, that when Bagehot died he " carried away into the next world more originality of thought than is now to be found in the three Estates of the Realm."

An epitome of Bagehot's life can be given very briefly. He was born in February, 1826, and died in March, 1877, — the month in which one would prefer to die. Between those two dates he had much quaint experience as a boy, and much sober business experience as a man. He wrote essays on poets, prose writers, statesmen, whom he would, with abundant insight, but without too much respect of persons; also books on banking, on the early development of society, and on English politics, kindling a flame of interest with these dry materials such as made men stare who had often described the facts of society themselves, but who had never dreamed of applying fire to them, as Bagehot did, to make them give forth light and wholesome heat. He set the minds of a few fortunate friends aglow with the delights of the very wonderful tongue which nature had given him through his mother. And then he died, while his power was yet young. Not a life of event or adventure, but a life of deep interest, none the less, because a life in which those two things of our modern life, commonly deemed incompatible, business and literature, namely, were combined without detriment to either; and from which, more interesting still, politics gained a profound expounder in one who was no politician and no party man, but, as he himself said, "between sizes in politics."

Mr. Bagehot was born in the centre of Somersetshire, that southwestern county of old England whose coast towns look across Bristol Channel to the highlands of Wales: a county of small farms, and pastures that keep their promise of fatness to many generous milkers; a county broken into abrupt hills, and sodden moors hardly kept from the inroads of the sea, as well as rural valleys open to the sun; a county visited by mists from the sea, and bathed in a fine soft atmosphere all its own; visited also by people of fashion, for it contains Bath; visited now also by those who have read Lorna Doone, for within it lies part of that Exmoor Forest in which stalwart John Ridd lived and wrought his mighty deeds of strength and love: a land which the Celts kept for long against both Saxon and Roman, but which Christianity easily conquered, building Wells Cathedral and the monastery at Glastonbury. Nowhere else, in days of travel, could Bagehot find a land of so great delight save in the northwest corner of Spain, where a golden light lay upon everything, where the sea shone with a rare, soft lustre, and where there was a like varied coast-line to that he knew and loved at home. He called it " a sort of better Devonshire: " and Devonshire is Somersetshire, — only more so! The atmospheric effects of his county certainly entered the boy Bagehot, and colored the nature of the man. He had its glow, its variety, its richness, and its imaginative depth.

But better than a fair county is a good parentage, and that, too, Bagehot had ; just the parentage one would wish to have who desired to be a force in the world's thought. His father, Thomas Watson Bagehot, was for thirty years managing director and vice-president of Stuckey's Banking Company, one of the oldest and best of those sturdy joint-stock companies which have for so many years stood stoutly up alongside the Bank of England as managers of the vast English fortune. But he was something more than a banker. He was a man of mind, of strong liberal convictions in politics, and of an abundant knowledge of English history wherewith to back up his opinions. He was one of the men who think, and who think in straight lines; who see, and see things. His mother was a Miss Stuckey, a niece of the founder of the banking company. But it was not her connection with bankers that made her an invaluable mother. She had, besides beauty, a most lively and stimulating wit; such a mind as we most desire to see in a woman, — a mind that stirs without irritating you, that rouses but does not belabor, amuses and yet subtly instructs. She could preside over the young life of her son in such a way as at once to awaken his curiosity and set him in the way of satisfying it. She was brilliant company for a boy, and rewarding for a man. She had suggestive people, besides, among her kinsmen, into whose companionship she could bring her son. Bagehot had that for which no university can ever offer an equivalent, — the constant and intelligent sympathy of both his parents in his studies, and their companionship in his tastes. To his father's strength his mother added vivacity. He would have been wise, perhaps, without her; but he would not have been wise so delightfully.

Bagehot got his schooling in Bristol, his university training in London. In Bristol lived Dr. Prichard, his mother's brother-in-law, and author of a notable book on the Physical History of Men. From him Bagehot unquestionably got his bent towards the study of race origins and development. In London, Cobden and Bright were carrying on an important part of their great agitation for the repeal of the corn laws, and were making such speeches as it stirred and bettered young men to hear. Bagehot had gone to University Hall, London, rather than to Oxford or Cambridge, because his father was a Unitarian, and would not have his son submit to the religious tests then required at the great universities. But there can be no doubt that there was more to be had at University Hall in that day than at either Oxford or Cambridge. Oxford and Cambridge were still dragging the very heavy chains of a hindering tradition; the faculty of University Hall contained many thorough and some eminent scholars; what was more, University Hall was in London, and London itself was a quickening and inspiring teacher for a lad in love with both books and affairs, as Bagehot was. He could ask penetrating questions of his professors, and he could also ask questions of London, seek out her secrets of history, and so experience to the full the charm of her abounding life. In after years, though he loved Somersetshire and clung to it with a strong home-keeping affection, he could never stay away from London for more than six weeks at a time. Eventually he made it his place of permanent residence.

His university career over, Bagehot did what so many thousands of young graduates before him had done, — he studied for the bar; and then, having prepared himself to practice law, followed another large body of young men in deciding to abandon it. He joined his father in his business as ship-owner and banker in Somersetshire, and in due time took his place among the directors of

Stuckey's Company. For the rest of his life, this man, whom the world knows as a man of letters, was first of all a man of business. In his later years, however, he identified himself with what may be called the literary side of business by becoming editor of that great financial authority, the "London Economist." He had, so to say, married into this position. His wife was the daughter of the Rt. Hon. James Wilson, who was the mind and manager, as well as the founder of the "Economist." Wilson's death seemed to leave the great financial weekly by natural succession to Bagehot; and certainly natural selection never made a better choice. It was under Bagehot that the "Economist" became a sort of financial providence for business men on both sides of the Atlantic. Its sagacious prescience constituted Bagehot himself a sort of supplementary chancellor of the exchequer, the chancellors of both parties resorting to him with equal confidence and solicitude. His constant contact with London, and with the leaders of politics and opinion there, of course materially assisted him also to those penetrating judgments touching the structure and working of English institutions which have made his volume on the English Constitution and his essays on Bolingbroke and Brougham and Peel, on Mr. Gladstone and Sir

George Cornewall Lewis, the admiration and de-
spair of all who read them.

Those who know Bagehot only as the writer of
some of the most delightful and suggestive literary
criticisms in the language wonder that he should
have been an authority on practical politics ; those
who used to regard the " London Economist " as
omniscient, and who knew him only as the editor
of it, marvel that he dabbled in literary criticism,
and incline to ask themselves, when they learn of
his vagaries in that direction, whether he can have
been so safe a guide as they deemed him, after all ;
those who know him through his political writings
alone venture upon the perusal of his miscellaneous
essays with not a little surprise and misgiving that
their master should wander so far afield.   And yet
the whole Bagehot is the only Bagehot.   Each
part of the man is incomplete, not only, but a trifle
incomprehensible, also, without the other parts.
What delights us most in his literary essays is
their broad practical sagacity, so uniquely married
as it is with pure taste and the style of a rapid
artist in words.   What makes his financial and
political writings whole and sound is the scope of
his mind outside finance and politics, the validity
of his observation all around the circle of thought
and affairs.   He was the better critic for being a

competent man of business and a trusted financial authority. He was the more sure-footed in his political judgments because of his play of mind in other and supplementary spheres of human activity.

The very appearance of the man was a sort of outer index to the singular variety of capacity that has made him so notable a figure in the literary annals of England. A mass of black, wavy hair; a dark eye, with depths full of slumberous, playful fire; a ruddy skin that bespoke active blood, quick in its rounds; the lithe figure of an excellent horseman; a nostril full, delicate, quivering, like that of a blooded racer, — such were the fitting outward marks of a man in whom life and thought and fancy abounded; the aspect of a man of unflagging vivacity, of wholesome, hearty humor, of a ready intellectual sympathy, of wide and penetrative observation. It is no narrow, logical shrewdness or cold penetration that looks forth at you through that face, even if a bit of mockery does lurk in the privatest corner of the eye. Among the qualities which he seeks out for special praise in Shakespeare is a broad tolerance and sympathy for illogical and common minds. It seems to him an evidence of size in Shakespeare that he was not vexed with smallness, but was patient, nay, sympathetic even, in his portrayal of it. " If every one were

logical and literary," he exclaims, " how would there
be scavengers, or watchmen, or caulkers, or coopers?
A patient sympathy, a kindly fellow-feeling for the
narrow intelligence necessarily induced by narrow
circumstances, — a narrowness which, in some degrees, seems to be inevitable, and is perhaps more
serviceable than most things to the wise conduct of
life, — this, though quick and half-bred minds may
despise it, seems to be a necessary constituent in
the composition of manifold genius. ' How shall
the world be served?' asks the host in Chaucer.
We must have cart-horses as well as race-horses,
draymen as well as poets. It is no bad thing, after
all, to be a slow man and to have one idea a year.
You don't make a figure, perhaps, in argumentative
society, which requires a quicker species of thought,
but is that the worse ? "

One of the things which strike us most in Bagehot himself is his capacity to understand inferior
minds ; and there can be no better test of sound
genius. He stood in the midst of affairs, and knew
the dull duty and humdrum fidelity which make up
the equipment of the ordinary mind for business,
for the business which keeps the world steady in
its grooves and makes it fit for habitation. He
perceived quite calmly, though with an odd, sober
amusement, that the world is under the dominion,

in most things, of the average man, and the average man he knows. He is, he explains, with his characteristic covert humor, " a cool, common person, with a considerate air, with figures in his mind, with his own business to attend to, with a set of ordinary opinions arising from and suited to ordinary life. He can't bear novelty or originalities. He says, ' Sir, I never heard such a thing before in my life ; ' and he thinks this a *reductio ad absurdum.* You may see his taste by the reading of which he approves. Is there a more splendid monument of talent and industry than the 'Times'? No wonder that the average man — that any one — believes in it. . . . But did you ever see anything there you had never seen before ? . . . Where are the deep theories, and the wise axioms, and the everlasting sentiments which the writers of the most influential publication in the world have been the first to communicate to an ignorant species? Such writers are far too shrewd. . . . The purchaser desires an article which he can appreciate at sight, which he can lay down and say, ' An excellent article, very excellent ; exactly my own sentiments.' Original theories give trouble ; besides, a grave man on the Coal Exchange does not desire to be an apostle of novelties among the contemporaneous dealers in fuel ; he wants to be

provided with remarks he can make on the topics
of the day which will not be known not to be his,
that are not too profound, which he can fancy the
paper only reminded him of.   And just in the
same way," — thus he proceeds with the sagacious
moral, — " precisely as the most popular political
paper is not that which is abstractedly the best or
most instructive, but that which most exactly takes
up the minds of men where it finds them, catches
the floating sentiment of society, puts it in such a
form as society can fancy would convince another
society which did not believe, so the most influential of constitutional statesmen is the one who most
felicitously expresses the creed of the moment, who
administers it, who embodies it in laws and institutions, who gives it the highest life it is capable
of, who induces the average man to think, ' I could
not have done it any better if I had had time myself.' "

See how his knowledge of politics proceeds out
of his knowledge of men.   " You may talk of the
tyranny of Nero and Tiberius," he exclaims, " but
the real tyranny is, the tyranny of your next-door
neighbor.   What law is so cruel as the law of doing what he does?   What yoke is so galling as the
necessity of being like him?   What espionage of
despotism comes to your door so effectually as the

eye of the man who lives at your door? Public opinion is a permeating influence, and it exacts obedience to itself; it requires us to think other men's thoughts, to speak other men's words, to follow other men's habits. Of course, if we do not, no formal ban issues, no corporeal pain, the coarse penalty of a barbarous society, is inflicted on the offender, but we are called ' eccentric ; ' there is a gentle murmur of ' most unfortunate ideas,' ' singular young man,' ' well intentioned, I dare say, but unsafe, sir, quite unsafe.' The prudent, of course, conform."

There is, no doubt, a touch of mockery in all this, but there is unquestionable insight in it, too, and a sane knowledge also of the fact that dull, common judgments are, after all, the cement of society. It is Bagehot who says somewhere that it is only dull nations, like the Romans and the English, who can become or remain for any length of time self-governing nations, because it is only among them that duty is done through lack of knowledge sufficient or imagination enough to suggest anything else to do : only among them that the stability of slow habit can be had.

It would be superficial criticism to put forward Bagehot's political opinions as themselves the proof of his extraordinary power as a student and analyst of institutions.   His life, his broad range of study, his quick versatility, his shrewd appreciation of common men, his excursions through all the fields that men traverse in their thought of one another and in their contact with the world's business, — these are the soil out of which his political judgments spring, from which they get their sap and bloom.   In order to know institutions, you must know men ; you must be able to imagine histories, to appreciate characters radically unlike your own, to see into the heart of society and assess its notions, great and small.   Your average critic, it must be acknowledged, would be the worst possible commentator on affairs.   He has all the movements of intelligence without any of its reality.   But a man who sees authors with a Chaucerian insight into them as men, who knows literature as a realm of vital thought conceived by real men, of actual motive felt by concrete persons, this is a man whose opinions you may confidently ask, if not on current politics, at any rate on all that concerns the permanent relations of men in society.

It is for such reasons that one must first make known the most masterly of the critics of English political institutions as a man of catholic tastes and attainments, shrewdly observant of many kinds of men and affairs.   Know him once in this way, and his mastery in political thought is explained. If I were to make choice, therefore, of extracts from his works with a view to recommend him as a politician, I should choose those passages which show him a man of infinite capacity to see and understand men of all kinds, past and present. By showing in his case the equipment of a mind open on all sides to the life and thought of society, and penetrative of human secrets of many sorts, I should authenticate his credentials as a writer upon politics, which is nothing else than the public and organic life of society.

Examples may be taken almost at random. There is the passage on Sydney Smith, in the essay on the First Edinburgh Reviewers. We have all laughed with that great-hearted clerical wit ; but it is questionable whether we have all appreciated him as a man who wrote and wrought wisdom. Indeed, Sydney Smith may be made a very delicate test of sound judgment, the which to apply to friends of whom you are suspicious. There was a man beneath those excellent witticisms, a big, wholesome, thinking man ; but none save men of like wholesome natures can see and value his manhood and his mind at their real worth.

"Sydney Smith was an after-dinner writer. His words have a flow, a vigor, an expression, which is not given to hungry mortals. . . . There is little trace of labor in his composition; it is poured forth like an unceasing torrent, rejoicing daily to run its course. And what courage there is in it! There is as much variety of pluck in writing across a sheet as in riding across a country. Cautious men . . . go tremulously, like a timid rider; they turn hither and thither; they do not go straight across a subject, like a masterly mind. A few sentences are enough for a master of sentences. The writing of Sydney Smith is suited to the broader kind of important questions. For anything requiring fine nicety of speculation, long elaborateness of deduction, evanescent sharpness of distinction, neither his style nor his mind was fit. He had no patience for long argument, no acuteness for delicate precision, no fangs for recondite research. Writers, like teeth, are divided into incisors and grinders. Sydney Smith was a molar. He did not run a long, sharp argument into the interior of a question; he did not, in the common phrase, go deeply into it; but he kept it steadily under the contract of a strong, capable, jawlike understanding, — pressing its surface, effacing its intricacies, grinding it down. Yet this is done without toil. The play of the molar is instinctive and placid; he could not help it; it would seem that he had an enjoyment in it."

One reads this with a feeling that Bagehot both knows and likes Sydney Smith, and heartily appreciates him as an engine of Whig thought; and with the conviction that Bagehot himself, knowing thus and enjoying Smith's freehand method of writing, could have done the like himself, — could himself have made English ring to all the old Whig tunes, like an anvil under the hammer. And yet you have only to turn back a page in the same essay to find quite another Bagehot, — a Bagehot such as Sydney Smith could not have been. He is speaking of that other militant Edinburgh reviewer, Lord Jeffrey, and is recalling, as every one recalls, Jeffrey's review of Wordsworth's " Excursion." The first words of that review, as everybody remembers, were, " This will never do ; " and there followed upon those words, though not a little praise of the poetical beauties of the poem, a thoroughly meant condemnation of the school of poets of which Wordsworth was the greatest representative. Very celebrated in the world of literature is the leading case of Jeffrey *v.* Wordsworth. It is in summing up this case that Bagehot gives us a very different taste of his quality : —

" The world has given judgment. Both Mr. Wordsworth and Lord Jeffrey have received their reward. The one had his own generation, the laughter of men, the applause of drawing-rooms, the concurrence of the crowd ; the other a succeeding age, the fond enthusiasm of secret students, the lonely rapture of lonely minds.　And each has received according to his kind.　If all cultivated men speak differently because of the existence of Wordsworth and Coleridge ; if not a thoughtful English book has appeared for forty years without some trace for good or evil of their influence ; if sermon-writers subsist upon their thoughts ; if ' sacred poets ' thrive by translating their weaker portions into the speech of women ; if, when all this is over, some sufficient part of their writing will ever be found fitting food for wild musing and solitary meditation, surely this is because they possessed the inner nature, — ' an intense and glowing mind,' ' the vision and the faculty divine.'　But if, perchance, in their weaker moments, the great authors of the ' Lyrical Ballads ' did ever imagine that the world was to pause because of their verses, that ' Peter Bell ' would be popular in drawing-rooms, that ' Christabel ' would be perused in the city, that people of fashion would make a handbook of ' The Excursion,' it was well for them to be told at once that this was not so.　Nature ingeniously prepared a shrill artificial voice, which spoke in season and out of season, enough and more than enough, what will ever be the idea of the cities of the plain concerning those who live alone among the mountains, of the frivolous concerning the grave, of the gregarious concerning the recluse, of those who laugh concerning those who laugh not, of the common concerning the uncommon, of those who lend on usury concerning those who lend not ; the notion of the world of those whom it will not reckon among the righteous, — it said, 'This won't do!' And so in all time will the lovers of polished Liberalism speak concerning the intense and lonely prophet."

This is no longer the Bagehot who could " write across a sheet" with Sydney Smith. It is now a Bagehot whose heart is turned away from the cudgeling Whigs to see such things as are hidden from the bearers of cudgels, and revealed only to those who can await in the sanctuary of a quiet mind the coming of the vision.

Single specimens of such a man's writing do not suffice, of course, even as specimens. They need their context to show their appositeness, the full body of the writing from which they are taken to show the mass and system of the thought. Even separated pieces of his matter prepare us, nevertheless, for finding in Bagehot keener, juster estimates of difficult historical and political characters than it is given the merely exact historian, with his head full of facts and his heart purged of all imagination, to speak.   There is his estimate of the cavalier, for example : " A cavalier is always young.   The buoyant life arises before us, rich in hope, strong in vigor, irregular in action: men young and ardent, 'framed in the prodigality of nature ; ' open to every enjoyment, alive to every passion, eager, impulsive ; brave without discipline, noble without principle ; prizing luxury, despising danger ; capable of high sentiment, but in each of whom the

> ' addiction was to courses vain ;
> His companies unlettered, rude, and shallow ;
> His hours filled up with riots, banquets, sports,
> And never noted in him any study,
> Any retirement, any sequestration
> From open haunts and popularity.'

The political sentiment is part of the character ; the essence of Toryism is enjoyment. . . . The way to keep up old customs is to enjoy old customs ; the way to be satisfied with the present state of things is to enjoy the present state of things.   Over the cavalier mind this world passes with a thrill of delight ; there is an exultation in a daily event, zest in the ' regular thing,' joy at an old feast."

  Is it not most natural that the writer of a passage like that should have been a consummate critic of politics, seeing institutions through men, the only natural way? It was as necessary that he should be able to enjoy Sydney Smith and recognize the seer in Wordsworth as that he should be able to conceive the cavalier life and point of view; and in each perception there is the same power. He is as little at fault in understanding men of his own day. What would you wish better than his celebrated character of a "constitutional statesman," for example? " A constitutional statesman is a man of common opinions and uncommon abilities." Peel is his example. " His opinions resembled the daily accumulating insensible deposits of a rich alluvial soil. The great stream of time flows on with all things on its surface; and slowly, grain by grain, a mould of wise experience is unconsciously left on the still, extended intellect. . . . The stealthy accumulating words of Peel seem like the quiet leavings of some outward tendency, which brought these, but might as well have brought others. There is no peculiar stamp, either, on the ideas. They might have been any one's ideas. They belong to the general diffused stock of observations which are to be found in the civilized world. . . . He insensibly takes in and imbibes the ideas of those around him.

If he were left in a vacuum, he would have no ideas."

What strikes one most, perhaps, in all these passages, is the realizing imagination which illuminates them. And it is an imagination with a practical character all its own. It is not a creating, but a conceiving imagination; not the imagination of the fancy, but the imagination of the understanding. Conceiving imaginations, however, are of two kinds. For the one kind the understanding serves as a lamp of guidance; upon the other the understanding acts as an electric excitant, a keen irritant. Bagehot's was evidently of the first kind; Carlyle's, conspicuously of the second. There is something in common between the minds of these two men as they conceive society. Both have a capital grip upon the actual; both can conceive without confusion the complex phenomena of society; both send humorous glances of searching insight into the hearts of men. But it is the difference between them that most arrests our attention. Bagehot has the scientific imagination, Carlyle the passionate. Bagehot is the embodiment of witty common sense; all the movements of his mind illustrate that vivacious sanity which he has himself called "animated moderation." Carlyle, on the other hand, conceives men and their motives too often with a hot intolerance; there is heat in his imagination, — a heat that sometimes scorches and consumes. Life is for him dramatic, full of fierce, imperative forces. Even when the world rings with laughter, it is laughter which, in his ears, is succeeded by an echo of mockery; laughter which is but a defiance of tears. The actual which you touch in Bagehot is the practical, operative actual of a world of workshops and parliaments, — a world of which workshops and parliaments are the natural and desirable products. Carlyle flouts at modern legislative assemblies as "talking shops," and yearns for action such as is commanded by masters of action; preaches the doctrine of work and silence in some thirty volumes octavo. Bagehot points out that prompt, crude action is the instinct and practice of the savage; that talk, the deliberation of assemblies, the slow concert of masses of men, is the cultivated fruit of civilization, nourishing to all the powers of right action in a society which is not simple and primitive, but advanced and complex. He is no more imposed upon by parliamentary debates than Carlyle is. He knows that they are stupid, and, so far as wise utterance goes, in large part futile, too. But he is not irritated, as Carlyle is, for, to say the fact, he sees more than Carlyle sees. He sees the force

and value of the stupidity. He is wise, along with
Burke, in regarding prejudice as the cement of
society. He knows that slow thought is the ballast
of a self-governing state. Stanch, knitted timbers
are as necessary to the ship as sails. Unless the
hull is conservative in holding stubbornly together
in the face of every argument of sea weather,
there'll be lives and fortunes lost. Bagehot can
laugh at unreasoning bias. It brings a merry
twinkle into his eye to undertake the good sport
of dissecting stolid stupidity. But he would not
for the world abolish bias and stupidity. He would
much rather have society hold together; much
rather see it grow than undertake to reconstruct it.
"You remember my joke against you about the
moon," writes Sydney Smith to Jeffrey; "d—n
the solar system — bad light — planets too distant
— pestered with comets — feeble contrivance;
could make a better with great ease." There was
nothing of this in Bagehot. He was inclined to be
quite tolerant of the solar system. He understood
that society was more quickly bettered by sympathy than by antagonism.

Bagehot's limitations, though they do not ob-
trude themselves upon your attention as his excel-
lencies do, are in truth as sharp-cut and clear
as his thought itself. It would not be just the

truth to say that his power is that of critical analysis only, for he can and does construct thought concerning antique and obscure systems of political life and social action. But it is true that he does not construct for the future. You receive stimulation from him and a certain feeling of elation. There is a fresh air stirring in all his utterances that is unspeakably refreshing. You open your mind to the fine influence, and feel younger for having been in such an atmosphere. It is an atmosphere clarified and bracing almost beyond example elsewhere. But you know what you lack in Bagehot if you have read Burke. You miss the deep eloquence which awakens purpose. You are not in contact with systems of thought or with principles that dictate action, but only with a perfect explanation.

You would go to Burke, not to Bagehot, for inspiration in the infinite tasks of self-government; though you would, if you were wise, go to Bagehot rather than to Burke if you wished to realize just what were the practical daily conditions under which those tasks were to be worked out.

Moreover, there is a deeper lack in Bagehot. He has no sympathy with the voiceless body of the people, with the "mass of unknown men." He conceives the work of government to be a work which is possible only to the instructed few. He

would have the mass served, and served with devotion, but he would trouble to see them attempt
to serve themselves. He has not the stout fibre
and the unquestioning faith in the right and capacity of inorganic majorities which make the democrat. He has none of the heroic boldness necessary
for faith in wholesale political aptitude and capacity.
He takes democracy in detail in his thought, and
to take it in detail makes it look very awkward
indeed.

And yet surely it would not occur to the veriest
democrat that ever vociferated the " sovereignty of
the people " to take umbrage at anything Bagehot
might chance to say in dissection of democracy.
What he says is seldom provokingly true. There
is something in it all that is better than a " saving
clause," and that is a saving humor. Humor ever
keeps the whole of his matter sound; it is an excellent salt that keeps sweet the sharpest of his say-
ings. Indeed, Bagehot's wit is so prominent among
his gifts that I am tempted here to enter a general
plea for wit as fit company for high thoughts and
weighty subjects. Wit does not make a subject
light; it simply beats it into shape to be handled
readily. For my part, I make free acknowledgment that no man seems to me master of his subject who cannot take liberties with it; who cannot

slap his propositions on the back and be hail-fellow
well met with them. Suspect a man of shallowness
who always takes himself and all that he thinks
seriously. For light on a dark subject commend
me to a ray of wit. Most of your solemn explana-
tions are mere farthing candles in the great ex-
panse of a difficult question. Wit is not, I admit,
a steady light, but ah! its flashes give you sudden
glimpses of unsuspected things such as you will
never see without it. It is the summer lightning,
which will bring more to your startled eye in an
instant, out of the hiding of the night, than you
will ever be at the pains to observe in the full blaze
of noon.

Wit is movement, is play of mind; and the
mind cannot get play without a sufficient play-
ground. Without movement outside the world of
books, it is impossible a man should see aught but
the very neatly arranged phenomena of that world.
But it is possible for a man's thought to be instructed by the world of affairs without the man
himself becoming a part of it. Indeed, it is exceedingly hard for one who is in and of it to hold
the world of affairs off at arm's length and observe
it. He has no vantage-ground. He had better for
a while seek the distance of books, and get his perspective. The literary politician, let it be distinctly

said, is a very fine, a very superior species of the
man thoughtful. He reads books as he would lis-
ten to men talk. He stands apart, and looks on,
with humorous, sympathetic smile, at the play of
policies. He will tell you for the asking what the
players are thinking about. He divines at once
how the parts are cast. He knows beforehand
what each act is to discover. He might readily
guess what the dialogue is to contain. Were you
short of scene-shifters, he could serve you admira-
bly in an emergency. And he is a better critic of
the play than the players.

Had I command of the culture of men, I should
wish to raise up for the instruction and stimulation
of my nation more than one sane, sagacious, penetrative critic of men and affairs like Walter Bagehot. But that, of course. The proper thesis to
draw from his singular genius is this: It is not the
constitutional lawyer, nor the student of the mere
machinery and legal structure of institutions, nor
the politician, a mere handler of that machinery,
who is competent to understand and expound government; but the man who finds the materials for
his thought far and wide, in everything that reveals
character and circumstance and motive. It is
necessary to stand with the poets as well as with
lawgivers; with the fathers of the race as well as

with your neighbor of to-day; with those who toil and are sick at heart as well as with those who prosper and laugh and take their pleasure; with the merchant and the manufacturer as well as with the closeted student; with the schoolmaster and with those whose only school is life; with the orator and with the men who have wrought always in silence; in the midst of thought and also in the midst of affairs, if you would really comprehend those great wholes of history and of character which are the vital substance of politics.

V.

In the middle of the last century two Irish adventurers crossed over into England in search of their fortunes. Rare fellows they were, bringing treasure with them; but finding it somehow hard to get upon the market: traders with a curious cargo, offering edification in exchange for a living, and concealing the best of English under a rich brogue. They were Edmund Burke and Oliver Goldsmith.

They did not cross over together: 't was no joint venture. They had been fellow students at Trinity College, Dublin; but they had not, so far as we can learn, known each other there. Each went his own way till they became comrades in the reign of Samuel Johnson at the Turk's Head Tavern. Burke stepped very boldly forth into the exposed paths of public life; Goldsmith plunged into the secret ways about Grub Street. The one gave us essays upon public questions incomparable for their reach of view and their splendid power of expression; the other gave us writings so exquisite for their delicacy, purity, and finish as to incline us to love him almost as much as those who knew him loved him. We could not easily have forgiven Ireland if she had *not* given us these men. The one had grave faults of temper ; the other was a reckless, roystering fellow, with a most irrepressible Irish disposition ; but how much less we should have known without Burke, how much less we should have enjoyed without Goldsmith ! They have conquered places for themselves in English literature from which we neither can nor would dislodge them. For their sakes alone we can afford to forgive Ireland all the trouble she has caused us.

There is no man anywhere to be found in the annals of Parliament who seems more thoroughly to belong to England than does Edmund Burke, indubitable Irishman though he was. His words, now that they have cast off their brogue, ring out the authentic voice of the best political thought of the English race. " If any man ask me," he cries, " what a free government is, I answer, that, for any practical purpose, it is what the people think so, — and that they, and not I, are the natural, lawful, and competent judges of the matter." " Abstract liberty, like other mere abstractions, is not to be found. Liberty adheres in some sensible object ;

and every nation has formed to itself some favorite point, which by way of eminence becomes the criterion of their happiness." These sentences, taken from his writings on American affairs, might serve as a sort of motto of the practical spirit of our race in affairs of government. Look further, and you shall see how his imagination presently illuminates and suffuses his maxims of practical sagacity with a fine blaze of insight, a keen glow of feeling, in which you recognize that other masterful quality of the race, its intense and elevated conviction. "My hold on the colonies," he declares, " is in the close affection which grows from common names, from kindred blood, from similar privileges, and equal protection. These are the ties which, though light as air, are as strong as links of iron. Let the colonies always keep the idea of their civil rights associated with your government, — they will cling and grapple to you, and no force under heaven will be of power to tear them from their allegiance. But let it once be understood that your government may be one thing and their privileges another, that these two things may exist without any mutual relation, — and the cement is gone, the cohesion is loosened, and everything hastens to decay and dissolution. So long as you have the wisdom to keep the sovereign power of this country as the sanctuary of liberty, the sacred temple consecrated to our common faith, wherever the chosen race and sons of England worship freedom, they will turn their faces towards you." " We cannot, I fear," he says proudly of the colonies, " we cannot falsify the pedigree of this fierce people, and persuade them that they are not sprung from a nation in whose veins the blood of freedom circulates. The language in which they would hear you tell them this tale would detect the imposition; your speech would betray you. An Englishman is the unfittest person on earth to argue another Englishman into slavery." Does not your blood stir at these passages? And is it not because, besides loving what is nobly written, you feel that every word strikes towards the heart of the things that have made your blood what it has proved to be in the history of our race?

These passages, it should be remembered, are taken from a speech in Parliament and from a letter written by Burke to his constituents in Bristol. He had no thought to make them permanent sentences of political philosophy. They were meant only to serve an immediate purpose in the advancement of contemporaneous policy. They were framed for the circumstances of the time. They speak out spontaneously amidst matter of the moment: and they could be matched everywhere throughout his pamphlets and public utterances. No other similar productions that I know of have this singular, and as it were inevitable, quality of permanency. They have emerged from the mass of political writings put forth in their time with their freshness untouched, their significance un-obscured, their splendid vigor unabated. It is this that we marvel at, that they should remain modern and timely, purged of every element and seed of decay. The man who could do this must needs arrest our attention and challenge our inquiry. We wish to account for him as we should wish to penetrate the secrets of the human spirit and know the springs of genius.

Of the public life of Burke we know all that we could wish. He became so prominent a figure in the great affairs of his day that even the casual observer cannot fail to discern the main facts of his career; while the close student can follow him year by year through every step of his service. But his private life was withdrawn from general scrutiny in an unusual degree. He manifested always a marked reserve about his individual and domestic affairs, deliberately, it would seem, shield-ing them from impertinent inquiry. He loved the privacy of life in a great city, where one may escape notice in the crowd and enjoy a grateful " freedom from remark and petty censure." " Though I have the honor to represent Bristol," he said to Boswell, " I should not like to live there ; I should be obliged to be *so much upon my good behavior.* In London a man may live in splendid society at one time, and in frugal retirement at another, without animadversion. There, and there alone, a man's house is truly his *castle*, in which he can be in perfect safety from intrusion whenever he pleases. I never shall forget how well this was expressed to me one day by Mr. Meynell: 'The chief advantage of London,' he said, 'is, that a man is always *so near his burrow.*'" Burke took to his burrow often enough to pique our curiosity sorely. This singular, high-minded adventurer had some queer companions, we know: questionable fellows, whose life he shared, perhaps with a certain Bohemian relish, without sharing their morals or their works. It seems as incongruous that such wisdom and public spirit as breathe through his writings should have come to his thought in such company as that an exquisite idyll like Goldsmith's " Vicar of Wakefield " should have been conceived and written in squalid garrets. But neither Burke nor Goldsmith had been born into such comrade-ships or such surroundings. Doubtless, as sometimes happens, their minds kept their first freshness, taking no taint from the world that touched them on every hand in their manhood, after their minds had been formed. Goldsmith, as everybody knows, remained an innocent all his life, a naïf and pettish boy amidst sophisticated men; and Burke too, notwithstanding his dignity and commanding intellectual habit, shows sometimes ·a touch of the same simplicity, a like habit of unguarded self-revelation. 'Twas their form, no doubt, of that impulsive and ingenuous quality which we observe in all Irishmen, and which we often mistake for simplicity. 'T was a flavor of their native soil. It was also something more and better than that, however. Not every Irishman displays such hospitality for direct and simple images of truth as these men showed, for that is characteristic only of the open and unsophisticated mind, — the mind that has kept pure and open eyes. Not that Burke always sees the truth; he is even deeply prejudiced often, and there are some things that he cannot see. But the passion that dominates him when he is wrong, as when he is right, is a natural passion, born with him, not acquired from a disingenuous world that mistakes interest for justice. His nature tells in everything. It is stock of his character which he contributes to the subjects his mind handles. He is trading always with the original treasure he brought over with him at the first. He has never impaired his genuineness, or damaged his principles.

Just where Burke got his generous constitution and predisposition to enlightened ways of thinking it is not easy to see. Certainly Richard Burke, his brother, the only other member of the family whose character we discern distinctly, had a quite opposite bent. The father was a steady Dublin attorney, a Protestant, and a man, so far as we know, of solid but not brilliant parts. The mother had been a Miss Nagle, of a Roman Catholic family, which had multiplied exceedingly in County Cork. Of the home and its life we know singularly little. We are told that many children were born to the good attorney, but we hear of only four of them that grew to maturity, Garret, Edmund, Richard, and a sister best known to Edmund's biographers as Mrs. French. Edmund, the second son, was born on the twelfth of January, 1729, in the second year of the reign of George II., Robert Walpole being chief minister of the Crown. How he fared or what sort of lad he was for the first twelve years of his life we have no idea. We only know that in the year 1741, being then twelve years old, he was sent with his brothers Garret and

Richard to the school of one Abraham Shackleton, a most capable and exemplary Quaker, at Ballytore, County Kildare, to get, in some two years' time, what he himself always accounted the best part of his education.   The character of the good master at Ballytore told upon the sensitive boy, who all his life through had an eye for such elevation and calm force of quiet rectitude as are to be seen in the best Quakers ; and with Richard Shackleton, the master's son, he formed a friendship from which no vicissitude of his subsequent career ever loosened his heart a whit.   All his life long the ardent, imaginative statesman, deeply stirred as he was by the momentous agitation of affairs, — swept away as he was from other friends, — retained his love for the grave, retired, almost austere, but generous and constant man who had been his favorite schoolfellow.   It is but another evidence of his un- failing regard for whatever was steady, genuine, and open to the day in character and conduct.

At fourteen he left Ballytore and was entered at Trinity College, Dublin.   Those were days when youths went to college tender, before they had be- come too tough to take impressions readily.   But Burke, even at that callow age, cannot be said to have been teachable.   He learned a vast deal, in- deed, but he did not learn much of it from his nominal masters at Trinity. Apparently Master Shackleton, at Ballytore, had enabled him to find his own mind. His four years at college were years of wide and eager reading, but not years of systematic and disciplinary study. With singular, if not exemplary, self-confidence, he took his education into his own hands. He got at the heart of books through their spirit, it would seem, rather than through their grammar. He sought them out for what they could yield him in thought, rather than for what they could yield him in the way of exact scholarship. That this boy should have had such an appetite for the world's literature, old and new, need not surprise us. Other lads before and since have found big libraries all too small for them. What should arrest our attention is, the law of mind disclosed in the habits of such lads : the quick and various curiosity of original minds, and particularly of imaginative minds. They long for matter to expand themselves upon : they will climb any dizzy height from which an exciting prospect is promised : it is their joy by some means to see the world of men and affairs. Burke set out as a boy to see the world that is contained in books ; and in his journeyings he met a man after his own heart in Cicero, the copious orator and versatile man of affairs, — the only man at all like

Burke for richness, expansiveness, and variety of
mind in all the ancient world. Cicero he conned
as his master and model. And then, having had
his fill for the time of discursive study and having
completed also his four years of routine, he was
graduated, taking his degree in the spring of 1748.

His father had entered him as a student at the
Middle Temple in 1747, meaning that he should
seek the prizes of his profession in England rather
than in the little world at home; but he did not take
up his residence in London until 1750, by which
time he had attained his majority. What he did
with the intervening two years, his biographers do
not at all know, and it is idle to speculate, being
confident, as we must, that he quite certainly did
whatever he pleased. He did the same when he
went up to London to live his terms at the Temple.
"The law," he declared to Parliament more than
twenty years afterwards, "is, in my opinion, one
of the first and noblest of human sciences, — a
science which does more to quicken and invigorate
the understanding than all other kinds of learning
put together; but it is not apt, except in persons
very happily born, to open and to liberalize the
mind exactly in the same proportion;" and, although himself a person "very happily born" in
respect of all natural powers, he felt that the life

of a lawyer would inevitably confine his roving mind within intolerably narrow limits. He learned the law, as he learned everything else, with an eye to discovering its points of contact with affairs, its intimate connections with the structure and functions of human society ; and, studying it thus, he made his way to so many of its secrets, won so firm a mastery of its central principles, as always to command the respect and even the admiration of lawyers. But the good attorney in Dublin was sorely disappointed. This was not what he had wanted. The son in whom he had centred his hopes preferred the life of the town to systematic study in his chambers ; wrote for the papers instead of devoting himself to the special profession he had been sent to master. "Of his leisure time," said the "Annual Register" just after his death, "of his leisure time much was spent in the company of Mrs. Woffington, a celebrated actress, whose conversation was not less sought by men of wit and genius than by men of pleasure."

We know very little about the life of Burke for the ten years, 1750–60, his first ten years in England, — except that he did *not* diligently apply himsely to his nominal business, the study of the law; and between the years 1752 and 1757 his biographers can show hardly one authentic trace of

his real life. They know neither his whereabouts
nor his employments. Only one scrap of his correspondence remains from those years to give us any
hint of the time. Even Richard Shackleton, his
invariable confidant and bosom friend, hears never
a word from him during that period, and is told
afterwards only that his correspondent has been
" sometimes in London, sometimes in remote parts
of the country, sometimes in France," and will
" shortly, please God, be in America." He disap-
pears a poor law student, under suspicion of his
father for systematic neglect of duty ; when he re-
appears he is married to the daughter of a worthy
physician and is author of two philosophical works
which are attracting a great deal of attention. We
have reason to believe that, in the mean time, he
did as much writing as they would take for the
booksellers ; we know that he frequented the London theatres and several of the innumerable debating clubs with which nether London abounded,
whetting his faculties, it is said, upon those of a certain redoubtable baker. He haunted the galleries
and lobbies of the House of Commons. His health
showed signs of breaking, and Dr. Nugent took him
from his lodgings in the Temple to his own house
and allowed him to fall in love with his daughter.
Partly for the sake of his health, perhaps, but more

particularly, no doubt, for the sake of satisfying an eager mind and a restless habit, he wandered off to " remote parts of the country " and to France, with one William Burke for company, a man either related to him or not related to him, he did not himself know which. In 1755, a long-suffering patience at length exhausted, his father shut the home treasury against him ; and then, — 't was the next year, — he published two philosophical works and married Miss Nugent.

One might say, no doubt, that this is an intelligible enough account of a young fellow's life between twenty and thirty : and that we can fill in the particulars for ourselves. We have known other young Irishmen of restless and volatile natures, and need make no mystery of this one. Goldsmith, too, disappeared, we remember, in that same decade, making show of studying medicine in Edinburgh, but not really studying it, and then wandering off to the Continent, and going it afoot in light-hearted, happy-go-lucky fashion through the haunts both of the gay Latin races and the sad Teutonic, greatly to the delectation, no doubt, of the natives, — for all the world loves an innocent Irishman, with his heart upon his sleeve. 'T would all be very plain indeed if we found in Burke that light-hearted vein. But we do not.

The fellow is sober and strenuous from the first, studying the things he was not sent to study with even too intent application, to the damage of his health, and looking through the pleasures of the town to the heart of the nation's affairs. He was a grave youth, evidently, gratifying his mind rather than his senses in the pleasures he sought; and when he emerges from obscurity it is first to give us a touch of his quality in the matter of intellectual amusement, and then to turn at once to the serious business of the discussion of affairs to which the rest of his life was to be devoted.

The two books which he gave the world in 1756 were "A Vindication of Natural Society," a satirical piece in the manner of Bolingbroke, and " A Philosophical Inquiry into the Origin of Our Ideas of the Sublime and Beautiful," which he had begun when he was nineteen and had since reconsidered and revised. Bolingbroke, not finding revealed religion to his taste, had written a " Vindication of Natural Religion " which his vigorous and elevated style and skillful dialectic had done much to make plausible. Burke put forth his " Vindication of Natural Society " as a posthumous work of the late noble lord, and so skillfully veiled the satirical character of the imitation as wholly to deceive some very grave critics, who thought they could discern Bolingbroke's flavor upon the tasting. For the style, too, they took to be unmistakably Bolingbroke's own. It had all his grandeur and air of distinction : it had his vocabulary and formal outline of phrase. The imitation was perfect. And yet if you will scrutinize it, the style is not Bolingbroke's, except in a trick or two, but Burke's. It seems Bolingbroke's rather because it is cold and without Burke's usual moral fervor than because it is rich and majestic and various. There is no great formal difference between Burke's style and Bolingbroke's : but there is a great moral and intellectual difference. When Burke is not in earnest there is perhaps no important difference at all. And in the " Vindication of Natural Society " Burke is not in earnest. The book is not, indeed, a parody, and its satirical quality is much too covert to make it a successful satire. Much that Burke urges against civil society he could urge in good faith, and his mind works soberly upon it. It is only the main thesis that he does not seriously mean. The rest he might have meant as Bolingbroke would have meant it.

The essay on The Sublime and Beautiful, though much admired by so great a master as Lessing, has not worn very well as philosophy. It is full, however, of acute and interesting observations, and is

adorned in parts with touches of rich color put on
with the authentic strokes of a master. We preserve it, perhaps, only because Burke wrote it;
and yet when we read it we feel inclined to pronounce it worth keeping for its own sake.

Both these essays were apprentice work. Burke
was trying his hand. They make us the more
curious about the conditions of what must have
been a notable apprenticeship. Young Burke
must have gone to school to the world in a way
worth knowing. But we cannot know, and that's
the end on't. Probably even William Burke,
Edmund's companion, could give us no very satisfactory account of the matter. The explanation
lay in what he thought and not in what he did as
he knocked about the world.

The company Burke kept was as singular as his
talents, though scarcely so eminent. *We* speak of
" Burke," but the London of his day spoke of " the
Burkes," meaning William, who may or may not
have been Edmund's kinsman, Edmund himself,
and Richard, Edmund's younger brother, who had
followed him to London to become, to say truth, an
adventurer emphatically not of the elevated sort.
Edmund was destined to become the leader of England's thought in more than one great matter of
policy, and has remained a master among all who

think profoundly upon public affairs; but William was for long the leader and master of " the Burkes." He was English born; had been in Westminster School; and had probably just come out from Christ Church, Oxford, when he became the companion of Edmund's wanderings. He was a man of intellect and literary power enough to be deemed the possible author of the " Letters of Junius; " he was born moreover with an eye for the ways of the world, and could push his own fortunes with an unhesitating hand. It was he who first got public office, and it was he who formed the influential connections which got Edmund into Parliament. He himself entered the House at the same time, and remained there, a useful party member, for some eight years. He made those from whom he sought favors dislike him for his audacity in demanding the utmost, and more than the utmost, that he could possibly hope to get; but he seems to have made those whom he served love him with a very earnest attachment. He was self-seeking; but he was capable of generosity, to the point of self-sacrifice even, when he wished to help his friend. He early formed a partnership with Richard Burke in immense stock-jobbing speculations in the securities of the East India Company; but he also formed a literary partnership with Edmund in the preparation of a sketch of the European settlements in America, and made himself respected as a strong party writer in various pamphlets on questions of the day. He could unite the two brothers by speculating with the one and thinking with the other.

Such were " the Burkes." Edmund's home was always the home also of the other two, whenever they wished to make it so; the strongest personal affection, avowed always by Edmund with his characteristic generous warmth, bound the three men together; their purses they had in common. Edmund was not expected, apparently, to take part in the speculations which held William and Richard together; something held him aloof to which they consented, — some natural separateness of mind and character which they evidently accepted and respected. There can hardly be said to have been any aloofness of *disposition* on Edmund's part. There is something in an Irishman, — even in an Irishman who holds himself to the strictest code of upright conduct, — which forbids his acting as moral censor upon others. He can love a man none the less for generous and manly qualities because that man does what he himself would not do. Burke, moreover, had an easy standard all his life about accepting money favors. He seems to have felt somehow that his intense and wholehearted devotion to his friends justified gifts and forgiven loans of money from them. He shared the prosperity of his kinsmen without compunction, using what he got most liberally for the assistance of others ; and when their fortunes came to a sudden ruin, he helped them with what he had. We ought long ago to have learned that the purest motives and the most elevated standards of conduct may go along with a singular laxness of moral detail in some men ; and that such characters will often constrain us to love them to the point of justifying everything that they ever did. Edmund Burke's close union with William and Richard does not present the least obstacle to our admiration for the noble qualities of mind and heart which he so conspicuously possessed, or make us for a moment doubt the thorough disinterestedness of his great career.

Burke's marriage was a very happy one. Mrs. Burke's thoroughly sweet temperament acted as a very grateful and potent charm to soothe her husband's mind when shaken by the agitations of public affairs ; her quiet capacity for domestic management relieved him of many small cares which might have added to his burdens. Her affection satisfied his ardent nature. He speaks of her in his will as " my entirely beloved and incomparable wife," and every glimpse we get of their home life confirms the estimate. After his marriage the most serious part of his intellectual life begins ; the commanding passion of his mind is disclosed. He turns away from philosophical amusements to public affairs. In 1757 appeared " An Account of the European Settlements in America," which William Burke had doubtless written, but which Edmund had almost certainly radically revised ; and Edmund himself published the first part of " An Abridgment of the History of England" which he never completed. In 1758, he proposed to Dodsley, the publisher, a yearly volume, to be known as the " Annual Register," which should chronicle and discuss the affairs of England and the Continent. It was the period of the Seven Years' War, which meant for England a sharp and glorious contest with France for the possession of America. Burke was willing to write the annals of the critical year 1758 for a hundred pounds ; and so, in 1759, the first volume of the " Annual Register " appeared ; and the plan then so wisely conceived has yielded its annual volume to the present day. Burke never acknowledged his connection with this great work, — he never publicly recognized anything he had done upon contract for the publishers, — but it is quite certain that for very many years his was the presiding and planning mind in the production of the " Register." For the first few years of its life he probably wrote the whole of the record of events with his own hand. It was a more useful apprenticeship than that in philosophy. It gave him an intimate acquaintance with affairs which must have served as a direct preparation for the great contributions he was destined to make to the mind and policy of the Whig party.

But this, even in addition to other hack work for the booksellers, did not keep Burke out of pecuniary straits. He sought, but failed to get, an appointment as consul at Madrid, using the interest of Dr. Markham, William's master at Westminster School ; and then he engaged himself as a sort of private secretary or literary attendant to William Gerard Hamilton, whom he served, apparently to the almost entire exclusion of all other employments, for some four years, going with him for a season to Ireland, where Hamilton for a time held the appointment of Secretary to the Lord Lieutenant. Hamilton is described by one of Burke's friends as " a sullen, vain, proud, selfish, cankered-hearted, envious reptile," and Mr. Morley says that there is " not a word too many nor too strong in the description." At any rate, Burke's proud spirit presently revolted from further service, and he threw up a pension of three hundred pounds which Hamilton had obtained for him rather than retain any connection with the man, or remain under any sort of obligation to him. In the mean time, however, his relations with Hamilton had put him in the way of meeting many public men of weight and influence, and he had gotten his first direct introduction to the world of affairs.

It was 1764 when he shook himself free from this connection. 1764 is a year to be marked in English literary annals. It was in the spring of that year that that most celebrated of literary clubs was formed at the Turk's Head Tavern, Gerrard Street, Soho, by notable good company : Dr. Johnson, Garrick, Sir Joshua Reynolds, Goldsmith, Sheridan, Gibbon, Dr. Barnard, Beauclerk, Langton, — we know them all; for has not Boswell given us the freedom of the Club and made us delighted participants in its conversations and diversions? Into this company Burke was taken at once. His writings had immediately attracted the attention of such men as these, and had promptly procured him an introduction into literary society. His powers told nowhere more brilliantly than in conversation. "It is when you come close to a man in conversation," said Dr. Johnson, "that you discover what his real abilities are. To make a

speech in an assembly is a sort of knack. Now
I honor Thurlow; Thurlow is a fine fellow, he
fairly puts his mind to yours." There can be no
disputing the dictum of the greatest master of conversation : and the admirer of Burke must be willing to accept it, at any rate for the nonce, for
Johnson admitted that Burke invariably put him
on his mettle. " That fellow," he exclaimed, "calls
forth all my powers!" "Burke's talk," he said,
"is the ebullition of his mind; he does not talk
from a desire of distinction, but because his mind
is full; he is never humdrum, never unwilling to
talk, nor in haste to leave off." The redoubtable
doctor loved a worthy antagonist in the great game
of conversation, and he always gave Burke his un-
grudging admiration. When he lay dying, Burke
visited his bedside, and, finding Johnson very
weak, anxiously expressed the hope that his presence cost him no inconvenience. " I must be in a
wretched state indeed," cried the great-hearted old
man, "when your company would not be a delight
to me." It was short work for Burke to get the
admiration of the company at the Turk's Head.
But he did much more than that: he won their devoted affection. Goldsmith said that Burke wound
his way into a subject like a serpent; but he made
his way straight into the hearts of his friends.

His powers are all of a piece : his heart is inextricably mixed up with his mind : his opinions are immediately transmuted into convictions : he does not talk for distinction, because he does not use his mind for the mere intellectual pleasure of it, but because he also deeply feels what he thinks. He speaks without calculation, almost impulsively.

That is the reason why we can be so sure of the essential purity of his nature from the character of his writings. They are not purely intellectual productions : there is no page of abstract reasoning to be found in Burke. His mind works upon concrete objects, and he speaks always with a certain passion, as if his affections were involved. He is irritated by opposition, because opposition in the field of affairs, in which his mind operates, touches some interest that is dear to him. Noble generalizations, it is true, everywhere broaden his matter : there is no more philosophical writer in English in the field of politics than Burke. But look, and you shall see that his generalizations are never derived from abstract premises. The reasoning is upon familiar matter of to-day. He is simply taking questions of the moment to the light, holding them up to be seen where great principles of conduct may shine upon them from the general experience of the race. He is not constructing systems of thought, but simply stripping thought of its accidental features. He is even deeply impatient of abstractions in political reasoning, so passionately is he devoted to what is practicable, and fit for wise men to do. To know such a man is to experience all the warmer forces of the mind, to feel the generous and cheering heat of character; and all noble natures will love such a man, because of kinship of quality. All noble natures that came close to Burke did love him and cherish their knowledge of him. They loaned him money without stint, and then forgave him the loans, as if it were a privilege to help him, and no way unnatural that he should never return what he received, finding his spirit made for fraternal, not for commercial relations.

It is pleasing, as it is also a little touching, to see how his companions thus freely accorded to Burke the immunities and prerogatives of a prince amongst them. No one failed to perceive how large and imperial he was, alike in natural gifts and in the wonderful range of his varied acquirements. Sir James Mackintosh, though he very earnestly combated some of Burke's views, intensely admired his greatness. He declared that Gibbon " might have been taken from a corner of Burke's mind without ever being missed." " A wit said of Gibbon's ' Autobiography ' that he did not know the difference between himself and the Roman Empire. He has narrated his ' progressions from London to Buriton and from Buriton to London ' in the same monotonous, majestic periods that he recorded the fall of states and empires." And we certainly feel a sense of incongruity : the two subjects, we perceive, are hardly commensurable. Perhaps in Burke's case we should have felt differently, — we *do* feel differently. In that extraordinary " Letter to a Noble Lord," in which he defends his pension so proudly against the animadversions of the Duke of Bedford, how magnificently he speaks of his services to the country ; how proud and majestic a piece of autobiography it is! How insignificant does the ancient house of Bedford seem, with all its long generations, as compared with this single and now lonely man, without distinguished ancestry or hope of posterity ! He speaks grandly about himself, as about everything ; and yet I see no disparity between the subject and the manner !

Outside the small circle of those who knew and loved him, his generation did not wholly perceive this. There seemed a touch of pretension in this proud tone taken by a man who had never held high office or exercised great power. He had made great speeches, indeed, no one denied that ; he had written great party pamphlets, — that everybody knew; his had been the intellectual force within the group of Whigs that followed Lord Rockingham, — that, too, the world in general perceived and acknowledged; and when he died, England knew the man who had gone to be a great man. But, for all that, his tone must, in his generation, have seemed disproportioned to the part he had played. His great authority is over us rather than over the men of his own day.

Burke had the thoughts of a great statesman, and uttered them with unapproachable nobility; but he never wielded the power of a great statesman. He was kept always in the background in active politics, in minor posts, and employed upon subordinate functions. This would be a singular circumstance, if there were any novelty in it; but the practice of keeping men of insignificant birth out of the great offices was a practice which had "broadened down from precedent to precedent" until it had become too strong for even Burke to breast or stem. Perhaps, too, there were faults of temper which rendered Burke unfit to exercise authority in directing the details, and determining the practical measures, of public policy : — but we shall look into that presently.

In July, 1765, the Marquis of Rockingham

became prime minister of England, and Burke became his private secretary. He owed his introduction to Lord Rockingham, as usual, to the good offices of William Burke, who seems to have found means of knowing everybody it was to the interest of " the Burkes " to know. A more fortunate connection could hardly have been made. Lord Rockingham, though not a man of original powers, was a man of the greatest simplicity and nobleness of character, and, like most upright men, knew how to trust other men. He gave Burke immediate proof of his manly qualities. The scheming old Duke of Newcastle, who ought to have been a connoisseur in low men, mistook Burke for one. Shocked that this obscurely born and unknown fellow should be accorded confidential relations by Lord Rockingham, he hurried to his lordship with an assortment of hastily selected slanders against Burke. His real name, he reported, was O'Bourke; he was an Irish adventurer without character, and a rank Papist to boot; it would ruin the administration to have such a man connected with the First Lord of the Treasury. Rockingham, with great good sense and frankness, took the whole matter at once to Burke; was entirely satisfied by Burke's denials; and admitted him immediately to intimate relations of warm personal friendship

which only death broke off. William Burke obtained for himself an Undersecretaryship of State
and arranged with Lord Verney, at that time his
partner in East India speculations, that two of his
lordship's parliamentary boroughs should be put
at his and Edmund's disposal. Edmund Burke,
accordingly, entered Parliament for the borough
of Wendover on the 14th of January, 1766, at ι
the age of thirty-seven, and in the first vigor of
his powers.

"Now we who know Burke," announced Dr.
Johnson, "know that he will be one of the first
men in the country." Burke promptly fulfilled
the prediction. He made a speech before he had
been in the House two weeks; a speech that made
him at once a marked man. His health was now
firmly established; he had a commanding physique;
his figure was tall and muscular, and his bearing
full of a dignity which had a touch almost of haugh-
tiness in it. Although his action was angular and
awkward, his extraordinary richness and fluency of
utterance drew the attention away from what he
was doing to what he was saying. His voice was
harsh, and did not harmonize with the melodious
measures in which his words poured forth; but it
was of unusual compass, and carried in it a sense
of confidence and power. His utterance was too

rapid, his thought bore him too impulsively forward, but the pregnant matter he spoke "filled the
town with wonder." The House was excited by
new sensations. Members were astonished to recognize a broad philosophy of politics running
through this ardent man's speeches. They felt the
refreshment of the wide outlook he gave them, and
were conscious of catching glimpses of excellent
matter for reflection at every turn of his hurrying
thought. They wearied of it, indeed, after a while:
the pace was too hard for most of his hearers, and
they finally gave over following him when the
novelty and first excitement of the exercise had
worn off. He too easily lost sight of his audience
in his search for principles, and they resented his
neglect of them, his indifference to their tastes.
They felt his lofty style of reasoning as a sort of
rebuke, and deemed his discursive wisdom out of
place amidst their own thoughts of imperative personal and party interest. He had, before very
long, to accustom himself, therefore, to speak to an
empty House and subsequent generations. His
opponents never, indeed, managed to feel quite
easy under his attacks: his arrows sought out their
weak places to the quick, and they winced even
when they coughed or seemed indifferent; but they
comforted themselves with the thought that the

orator was also tedious and irritating to his own friends, teasing them too with keen rebukes and vexatious admonitions. The high and wise sort of speaking must always cause uneasiness in a political assembly. The more equal and balanced it is, the more must both parties be threatened with reproof.

I would not be understood as saying that Burke's speeches were impartial. They were not. He had preferences which amounted to prejudices. He was always an intense party man. But then he was a party man with a difference. He believed that the interests of England were bound up with the fortunes of the Rockingham Whigs; but he did not separate the interests of his party and the interests of his country. He cherished party connections because he conceived them to be absolutely necessary for effective public service. " Where men are not acquainted with each other's principles," he said, " nor experienced in each other's talents, nor at all practiced in their mutual habitudes or dispositions by joint efforts in business; no personal confidence, no friendship, no common interest, subsisting among them; it is evidently impossible that they can act a public part with uniformity, perseverance, or efficacy. In a connection, the most inconsiderable man, by adding to the weight of the whole, has his value, and his use;

out of it, the greatest talents are wholly unservice-
able to the public." "When bad men combine,
the good must associate." " It is not enough in a
situation of trust in the commonwealth, that a man
means well to his country ; it is not enough that in
his single person he never did an evil act, but
always voted according to his conscience, and even
harangued against every design which he appre-
hended to be prejudicial to the interests of his
country. . . . Duty demands and requires, that
what is right should not only be made known, but
made prevalent; that what is evil should not only
be detected, but defeated. When the public man
omits to put himself in a situation of doing his
duty with effect, it is an omission that frustrates
the purposes of his trust almost as much as if he
had formally betrayed it." Burke believed the
Rockingham Whigs to be a combination of good
men, and he felt that he ought to sacrifice something to keep himself in their connection. He
regarded them as men who " believed private honor
to be the foundation of public trust; that friendship was no mean step towards patriotism ; that he
who, in the common intercourse of life, showed he
regarded somebody besides himself, when he came
to act in a public situation, might probably consult
some other interest than his own." He admitted

that such confederacies had often " a narrow, big-
oted, and proscriptive spirit ; " " but, where duty
renders a critical situation a necessary one," he
said, " it is our business to keep free from the evils
attendant upon it; and not to fly from the situation
itself. If a fortress is seated in an unwholesome
air, an officer of the garrison is obliged to be
attentive to his health, but he must not desert his
station." " A party," he declared, " is a body of
men united for promoting by their joint endeavors
the national interest upon some particular principle
in which they are all agreed." " Men thinking
freely, will," he very well knew, " in particular instances, think differently. But still as the greater
part of the measures which arise in the course of
public business are related to, or dependent on,
some great, *leading, general principles in government*, a man must be peculiarly unfortunate in the
choice of his political company, if he does not agree
with them at least nine times in ten. If he does
not concur in these general principles upon which
the party is founded, and which necessarily draw
on a concurrence in their application, he ought
from the beginning to have chosen some other,
more conformable to his opinions. When the
question is in its nature doubtful, or not very
material, the modesty which becomes an individual,

and that partiality which becomes a well-chosen
friendship, will frequently bring on an acquiescence
in the general sentiment. Thus the disagreement
will naturally be rare ; it will be only enough to
indulge freedom, without violating concord, or dis-
turbing arrangement."

Certainly there were no party prizes for Burke.
During much the greater part of his career the
party to which he adhered was in opposition ; and
even when in office it had only small favors for
him. Even his best friends advised against his
appointment to any of the great offices of state,
deeming him too intemperate and unpractical.
And yet the intensity of his devotion to his party
never abated a jot. Assuredly there was never a
less selfish allegiance. His devotion was for the
principles of his party, as he conceived and constructed them. It was a moral and intellectual
devotion. He had embarked all his spirit's fortunes in the enterprise. Faults he unquestionably
had, which seemed very grave. He was passionate
sometimes beyond all bounds : he seriously frightened cautious and practical men by his haste and
vehemence in pressing his views for acceptance.
He was capable of falling, upon occasion, into a
very frenzy of excitement in the midst of debate,
when he would often shock moderate men by the

ungoverned license of his language. But his friends were as much to blame for these outbreaks as he was. They cut him to the quick by the way in which they criticised and misunderstood him. His heart was maddened by the pain of their neglect of his just claims to their confidence. They seemed often to use him without trusting him, and their slights were intolerable to his proud spirit. Practically, and upon a narrow scale of expediency, they may have been right: perhaps he was *not* circumspect enough to be made a responsible head of administration. Unquestionably, too, they loved him and meant him no unkindness. But it was none the less tragical to treat such a man in such a fashion. They may possibly have temporarily served their country by denying to Burke full public acknowledgment of his great services; but they cruelly wounded a great spirit, and they hardly served mankind.

They did Burke an injustice, moreover. They greatly underrated his practical powers. In such offices as he was permitted to hold he showed in actual administration the same extraordinary mastery of masses of detail which was the foundation of his unapproachable mastery of general principles in his thinking. His thought was always immersed in matter, and concrete detail did not confuse him when he touched it any more than it did when he meditated upon it.   Immediate contact with affairs always steadied his judgment.   He was habitually temperate in the conduct of business.   It was only in speech and when debating matters that stirred the depths of his nature that he gave way to uncalculating fervor.   He was intemperate in his emotions, but seldom in his actions.   He could, and did, write calm state papers in the very midst and heat of parliamentary affairs that subjected him to the fiercest excitements.   He was eminently capable of counsel as well as of invective.

He served his party in no servile fashion, for all he adhered to it with such devotion.   He sacrificed his intellectual independence as little as his personality in taking intimate part in its counsels.   He gave it principles, indeed, quite as often as he accepted principles from it.   In the final efforts of his life, when he engaged every faculty of his mind in the contest that he waged with such magnificent wrath against the French revolutionary spirit, he gave tone to all English thought, and direction to many of the graver issues of international policy. Rejected oftentimes by his party, he has at length been accepted by the world.

His habitual identification with opposition rather than with the government gave him a certain advantage. It relaxed party discipline and indulged his independence. It gave leave, too, to the better efforts of his genius: for in opposition it is principles that tell, and Burke was first and last a master of principles. Government is a matter of practical detail, as well as of general measures; but the criticism of government very naturally becomes a matter of the application of general principles, as standards rather than as practical means of policy.

Four questions absorbed the energies of Burke's life and must always be associated with his fame. These were, the American war for independence; administrative reform in the English home government; reform in the government of India; and the profound political agitations which attended the French Revolution. Other questions he studied, deeply pondered, and greatly illuminated, but upon these four he expended the full strength of his magnificent powers. There is in his treatment of these subjects a singular consistency, a very admirable simplicity of standard. It has been said, and it is true, that Burke had no system of political philosophy. He was afraid of abstract system in political thought, for he perceived that questions of government are moral questions, and that questions of morals cannot always be squared with the rules of logic, but run through as many ranges of

variety as the circumstances of life itself. "Man
acts from adequate motives relative to his interest,"
he said, "and not on metaphysical speculations.
Aristotle, the great master of reasoning, cautions
us, and with great weight and propriety, against
this species of delusive geometrical accuracy in
moral arguments, as the most fallacious of all
sophistry." And yet Burke unquestionably had a
very definite and determinable system of thought,
which was none the less a system for being based
upon concrete, and not upon abstract premises.
It is said by some writers (even by so eminent a
writer as Buckle) that in his later years Burke's
mind lost its balance and that he reasoned as if he
were insane; and the proof assigned is, that he, a
man who loved liberty, violently condemned, not
the terrors only, — that of course, — but the very
principles of the French Revolution. But to reason
thus is to convict one's self of an utter lack of comprehension of Burke's mind and motives: as a very
brief examination of his course upon the four great
questions I have mentioned will show.

From first to last Burke's thought is conservative. Let his attitude with regard to America
serve as an example. He took his stand, as everybody knows, with the colonies, against the mother
country; but his object was not revolutionary.

He did not deny the legal right of England to tax the colonies (*we* no longer deny it ourselves), but he wished to preserve the empire, and he saw that to insist upon the right of taxation would be irrevocably to break up the empire, when dealing with such a people as the Americans. He pointed out the strong and increasing numbers of the colonists, their high spirit in enterprise, their jealous love of liberty, and the indulgence England had hitherto accorded them in the matter of self-government, permitting them in effect to become an independent people in respect of all their internal affairs; and he declared the result matter for just pride. "Whilst we follow them among the tumbling mountains of ice, and behold them penetrating into the deepest frozen recesses of Hudson's Bay and Davis's Straits," he exclaimed, in a famous passage of his incomparable speech on Conciliation with America, "whilst we are looking for them beneath the arctic circle, we hear that they have pierced into the opposite region of polar cold, that they are at the antipodes, and engaged under the frozen serpent of the South. Falkland Island, which seemed too remote and romantic an object for the grasp of national ambition, is but a stage and resting place in the progress of their victorious industry. Nor is the equinoctial heat more discouraging to them than the accumulated winter of both the poles. We know that whilst some of them draw the line and strike the harpoon on the coast of Africa, others run the longitude, and pursue their gigantic game along the coast of Brazil. No sea but what is vexed by their fisheries. No climate that is not witness to their toils. Neither the perseverance of Holland, nor the activity of France, nor the dexterous and firm sagacity of English enterprise, ever carried this most perilous mode of hardy industry to the extent to which it has been pushed by this recent people, — a people who are still, as it were, but in the gristle, and not yet hardened into the bone of manhood. When I contemplate these things, — when I know that the colonies in general owe little or nothing to any care of ours, and that they are not squeezed into this happy form by the constraints of watchful and suspicious government, but that, through a wise and salutary neglect, a generous nature has been suffered to take her own way to perfection, — when I reflect upon these effects, when I see how profitable they have been to us, I feel all the pride of power sink, and all the presumption in the wisdom of human contrivances melt and die away within me, — my rigor relents, — I pardon something to the spirit of liberty."

" I think it necessary," he insisted, " to consider distinctly the true nature and the peculiar circumstances of the object we have before us : because, after all our struggle, whether we will or not, we must govern America according to that nature and those circumstances, and not according to our own imaginations, not according to abstract ideas of right, by no means according to mere general theories of government, the resort to which appears to me, in our present situation, no better than arrant trifling." To attempt to force such a people would be a course of idle folly. Force, he declared, would not only be an odious " but a feeble instrument, for preserving a people so numerous, so active, so growing, so spirited as this, in a profitable and subordinate connection with " England.

" First, Sir," he cried, " permit me to observe, that the use of force alone is but *temporary*. It may subdue for a moment; but it does not remove the necessity of subduing again : and a nation is not governed which is perpetually to be conquered.

" My next objection is its *uncertainty*. Terror is not always the effect of force, and an armament is not a victory. If you do not succeed, you are without resource : for, conciliation failing, force remains ; but, force failing, no further hope of reconciliation is left. Power and authority are sometimes bought by kindness ; but they can never be begged as alms by an impoverished and defeated violence.

"A further objection to force is, that you *impair the object* by your very endeavors to preserve it. The thing you fought for is not the thing you recover, but depreciated, sunk, wasted, and consumed in the contest. Nothing less will content me than *whole America.* I do not choose to consume its strength along with our own; for in all parts it is the British strength I consume. . . . Let me add, that I do not choose wholly to break the American spirit ; because it is the spirit that has made the country.

" Lastly, we have no sort of *experience* in favor of force as an instrument in the rule of our colonies. Their growth and their utility has been owing to methods altogether different. Our ancient indulgence has been said to be pursued to a fault. It may be so ; but we know, if feeling is evidence, that our fault was more tolerable than our attempt to mend it, and our sin far more salutary than our penitence."

" Obedience is what makes government," " freedom, and not servitude, is the cure of anarchy," and you cannot insist upon one rule of obedience for Englishmen in America while you jealously maintain another for Englishmen in England. " For, in order to prove that the Americans have no right to their liberties, we are every day endeavoring to subvert the maxims which preserve the whole spirit of our own. To prove that the Americans ought not to be free, we are obliged to depreciate the value of freedom itself ; and we never seem to gain a paltry advantage over them in debate, without attacking some of those principles, or deriding some of those feelings, for which our ancestors have shed their blood." " The question with me is, not whether you have a right to render your people miserable, but whether it is not your interest to make them happy. It is not what a lawyer tells me I *may* do, but what humanity, reason, and justice tell me I *ought* to do. . . . Such is steadfastly my opinion of the absolute necessity of keeping up the concord of this empire by a unity of spirit, though in a diversity of operations, that, if I were sure that the colonists had, at their leaving this country, sealed a regular compact of servitude, that they had solemnly abjured all the rights of citizens, that they had made a vow to renounce all ideas of liberty for them and their posterity to all generations, yet I should hold myself obliged to conform to the temper I found universally prevalent in my own day, and to govern two million of men, impatient of servitude, on the principles of freedom. I am not determining a point of law; I am restoring tranquillity : and the general character and situation of a people must determine what sort of government is fitted for them. That point nothing else can or ought to determine." " All government, indeed every human benefit and enjoyment, every virtue and every prudent act, is founded on compromise and barter. We balance inconveniences ; we give and take; we remit some rights, that we may enjoy others ; and we choose rather to be happy citizens than subtle disputants." " Magnanimity in politics is not seldom the truest wisdom ; and a great empire and little minds go ill together."

Here you have the whole spirit of the man, and in part a view of his eminently practical system of thought. The view is completed when you advance with him to other subjects of policy. He pressed with all his energy for radical reforms in administration, but he earnestly opposed every change that might touch the structure of the constitution itself. He sought to secure the integrity of Parliament, not by changing the system of representation, but by cutting out all roots of corruption. He pressed forward with the most ardent in all plans of just reform, but he held back with the most conservative from all propositions of radical change. "To innovate is not to reform," he declared, and there is " a marked distinction between change and reformation. The former alters the substance of the objects themselves, and gets rid of all their essential good as well as of all the accidental evil annexed to them. Change is novelty ; and whether it is to operate any one of the effects of reformation at all, or whether it may not contradict the very principle upon which reformation is desired, cannot certainly be known beforehand. Reform is not a change in the substance or in the primary modification of the object, but a direct application of a remedy to the grievance complained of. So far as that is removed, all is sure. It stops there ; and if it fails, the substance which underwent the operation, at the very worst, is but where it was." This is the governing motive of his immense labors to accomplish radical economical reform in the administration of the government. He was not seeking economy merely ; to husband the resources of the country was no more than a means to an end, and that end was, to preserve the constitution in its purity. He believed that Parliament was not truly representative of the people because so many placemen found seats in it, and because so many members who might have been independent were bought by the too abundant favors of the Court. Cleanse Parliament of this corruption, and it would be restored to something like its pristine excellence as an instrument of liberty.

He dreaded to see the franchise extended and the House of Commons radically made over in its constitution. It had never been intended to be merely the people's House. It had been intended to hold all the elements of the state that were not to be found in the House of Lords or the Court. He conceived it to be the essential object of the constitution to establish a balanced and just intercourse between the several forces of an ancient society, and it was well that that balance should be preserved even in the House of Commons, rather than give perilous sweep to a single set of interests. " These opposed and conflicting interests," he said to his French correspondent, " which you considered as so great a blemish in your old and in our present Constitution, interpose a salutary check to all precipitate resolutions. They render deliberation a matter, not of choice, but of necessity ; they make all change a subject of *compromise*, which naturally begets moderation ; they produce *temperaments*, preventing the sore evil of harsh, crude, unqualified reformations, and rendering all the headlong exertions of arbitrary power, in the few

or in the many, forever impracticable. Through
that diversity of members and interests, general
liberty had as many securities as there are separate
views in the several orders; whilst by pressing
down the whole by the weight of a real monarchy,
the separate parts would have been prevented from
warping and starting from their allotted places."
" *We* wish," he said, " to derive all we possess *as
an inheritance from our forefathers.* Upon that
body and stock of experience we have taken care
not to inoculate any scion alien to the nature of the
original plant." " This idea of a liberal descent
inspires us with a sense of habitual native dignity,
which prevents that upstart insolence almost inevitably adhering to and disgracing those who are
the first acquirers of any distinction. By this
means our liberty becomes a noble freedom. It
carries an imposing and majestic aspect. It has a
pedigree and illustrating ancestors. It has its
bearings and its ensigns armorial. It has its gallery of portraits, its monumental inscriptions, its
records, evidences, and titles. We procure reverence to our civil institutions on the principle upon
which Nature teaches us to revere individual men :
on account of their age, and on account of those
from whom they are descended."

" When the useful parts of an old establishment

are kept, and what is superadded is to be fitted to what is retained, a vigorous mind, steady, persevering attention, various powers of comparison and combination, and the resources of an understanding fruitful in expedients are to be exercised; they are to be exercised in a continued conflict with the combined force of opposite vices, with the obstinacy that rejects all improvement, and the levity that is fatigued and disgusted with everything of which it is in possession. . . . Political arrangement, as it is a work for social ends, is to be only wrought by social means. There mind must conspire with mind. Time is required to produce that union of minds which alone can produce all the good we aim at. Our patience will achieve more than our force. If I might venture to appeal to what is so much out of fashion in Paris, — I mean to experience, — I should tell you that in my course I have known, and, according to my measure, have coöperated with great men; and I have never yet seen any plan which has not been mended by the observations of those who were much inferior in understanding to the person who took the lead in the business. By a slow, but well sustained progress, the effect of each step is watched; the good or ill success of the first gives light to us in the second; and so, from light to light,

we are conducted with safety, through the whole
series. . . . We are enabled to unite into a consistent whole the various anomalies and contending
principles that are found in the minds and affairs
of men. From hence arises, not an excellence in
simplicity, but one far superior, an excellence in
composition. Where the great interests of mankind are concerned through a long succession of
generations, that succession ought to be admitted
into some share in the counsels which are so deeply
to affect them."

It is not possible to escape deep conviction of
the wisdom of these reflections. They penetrate to
the heart of all practicable methods of reform.
Burke was doubtless too timid, and in practical
judgment often mistaken. Measures which in
reality would operate only as salutary and needed
reformations he feared because of the element of
change that was in them. He erred when he supposed that progress can in all its stages be made
without changes which seem to go even to the substance. But, right or wrong, his philosophy did
not come to him of a sudden and only at the end
of his life, when he found France desolated and
England threatened with madness for love of revolutionary principles of change. It is the key to
his thought everywhere, and through all his life.

It is the key (which many of his critics have never found) to his position with regard to the revolution in France. He was roused to that fierce energy of opposition in which so many have thought that they detected madness, not so much because of his deep disgust to see brutal and ignorant men madly despoil an ancient and honorable monarchy, as because he saw the spirit of these men cross the Channel and find lodgment in England, even among statesmen like Fox, who had been his own close friends and companions in thought and policy; not so much because he loved France as because he feared for England. For England he had Shakespeare's love:

> " That fortress built by nature for herself
> *Against infection and the hand of war ;*
> That happy breed of men, that little world,
> That precious stone set in the silver sea,
> Which serves it in the office of a wall,
> Or as a moat defensive to a house,
> *Against the envy of less happier lands ;*
> That blessed plot, that earth, that realm, that England."

'Twas to keep out infection and to preserve such precious stores of manly tradition as had made that little world " the envy of less happier lands " that Burke sounded so effectually that extraordinary alarm against the revolutionary spirit that was racking France from throne to cottage. Let us admit, if you will, that with reference to France herself he was mistaken. Let us say that when he admired the institutions which she was then sweeping away he was yielding to sentiment, and imagining France as perfect as the beauty of the sweet queen he had seen in her radiant youth. Let us concede that he did not understand the condition of France, and therefore did not see how inevitable that terrible revolution was: that in this case, too, the wages of sin was death. He was not defending France, if you look to the bottom of it; he was defending England: — and the things he hated are truly hateful. He hated the French revolutionary philosophy and deemed it unfit for free men. And that philosophy is in fact radically evil and corrupting. No state can ever be conducted on its principles. For it holds that government is a matter of contract and deliberate arrangement, whereas in fact it is an institute of habit, bound together by innumerable threads of association, scarcely one of which has been deliberately placed. It holds that the object of government is liberty, whereas the true object of government is justice; not the advantage of one class, even though that class constitute the majority, but right equity in the adjustment of the interests of all classes. It assumes that government can be made over at will, but assumes it without the slightest historical foundation. For governments have never been successfully and permanently changed except by slow modification operating from generation to generation. It contradicted every principle that had been so laboriously brought to light in the slow stages of the growth of liberty in the only land in which liberty had then grown to great proportions. The history of England is a continuous thesis against revolution; and Burke would have been no true Englishman, had he not roused himself, even fanatically, if there were need, to keep such puerile doctrine out.

If you think his fierceness was madness, look how he conducted the trial against Warren Hastings during those same years: with what patience, with what steadiness in business, with what temper, with what sane and balanced attention to detail, with what statesmanlike purpose! Note, likewise, that his thesis is the same in the one undertaking as in the other. He was applying the same principles to the case of France and to the case of India that he had applied to the case of the colonies. He meant to save the empire, not by changing its constitution, as was the method in France, and so shaking every foundation in order to dislodge an abuse, but by administering it uprightly and in a

liberal spirit. He was persuaded "that government was a practical thing, made for the happiness
of mankind, and not to furnish out a spectacle of
uniformity to gratify the schemes of visionary politicians. Our business," he said, "was to rule, not
to wrangle; and it would be a poor compensation
that we had triumphed in a dispute, whilst we had
lost an empire." The monarchy must be saved
and the constitution vindicated by keeping the
empire pure in all parts, even in the remotest
provinces. Hastings must be crushed in order
that the world might know that no English governor could afford to be unjust. Good government, like all virtue, he deemed to be a practical
habit of conduct, and not a matter of constitutional
structure. It is a great ideal, a thoroughly English
ideal; and it constitutes the leading thought of all
Burke's career.

In short, as I began by saying, this man, an
Irishman, speaks the best English thought upon the
essential questions of politics. He is thoroughly,
characteristically, and to the bottom English in all
his thinking. He is more liberal than Englishmen
in his treatment of Irish questions, of course; for
he understands them, as no Englishman of his
generation did. But for all that he remains the
chief spokesman for England in the utterance of

the fundamental ideals which have governed the action of Englishmen in politics. "All the ancient, honest, juridical principles and institutions of England," such was his idea, "are so many clogs to check and retard the headlong course of violence and oppression. They were invented for this one good purpose, that what was not *just* should not be *convenient.*" This is fundamental English doctrine. English liberty has consisted in making it unpleasant for those who were unjust, and thus getting them in the habit of being just for the sake of a *modus vivendi.* Burke is the apostle of the great English gospel of Expediency.

The politics of English-speaking peoples has never been speculative; it has always been profoundly practical and utilitarian. Speculative politics treats men and situations as they are supposed to be; practical politics treats them (upon no general plan, but in detail) as they are found to be at the moment of actual contact. With reference to America Burke argues: No matter what your legal right in the case, it is not *expedient* to treat America as you propose: a numerous and spirited people like the colonists will not submit; and your experiment will cost you your colonies. In the case of administrative reform, again, it is the higher sort of expediency he urges: If you wish to keep your government from revolution, keep it from corruption, and by making it pure render it permanent. To the French he says, It is not *expedient* to destroy thus recklessly these ancient parts of your constitution. How will you replace them? How will you conduct affairs at all after you shall have deprived yourselves of all balance and of all old counsel? It is both better and easier to reform than to tear down and reconstruct.

This is unquestionably the message of Englishmen to the world, and Burke utters it with incomparable eloquence. A man of sensitive imagination and elevated moral sense, of a wide knowledge and capacity for affairs, he stood in the midst of the English nation speaking its moral judgments upon affairs, its character in political action, its purposes of freedom, equity, wide and equal progress. It is the immortal charm of his speech and manner that gives permanence to his works. Though his life was devoted to affairs with a constant and unalterable passion, the radical features of Burke's mind were literary. He was a man of books, without being under the dominance of what others had written. He got knowledge out of books and the abundance of matter his mind craved to work its constructive and imaginative effects upon. It is singular how devoid of all direct references to books his writings are. The materials of his thought never reappear in the same form in which he obtained them. They have been smelted and recoined. They have come under the drill and inspiration of a great constructive mind, have caught life and taken structure from it. Burke is not literary because he takes from books, but because he makes books, transmuting what he writes upon into literature. It is this inevitable literary quality, this sure mastery of style, that mark the man, as much as his thought itself. He is a master in the use of the great style. Every sentence, too, is steeped in the colors of an extraordinary imagination. The movement takes your breath and quickens your pulses. The glow and power of the matter rejuvenate your faculties.

And yet the thought, too, is quite as imperishable as its incomparable vehicle.

> "The deepest, plainest, highest, clearest pen;
> The voice most echoed by consenting men;
> The soul which answered best to all well said
> By others, and which most requital made;
> Tuned to the highest key of ancient Rome,
> Returning all her music with his own;
> In whom, with nature, study claimed a part,
> And yet who to himself owed all his art."

VI.

THE TRUTH OF THE MATTER.

" GIVE us the facts, and nothing but the facts,"
is the sharp injunction of our age to its historians.
Upon the face of it, an eminently reasonable re-
quirement. To tell the truth simply, openly, without reservation, is the unimpeachable first principle
of all right dealing; and historians have no license
to be quit of it. Unquestionably they must tell us
the truth, or else get themselves enrolled among a
very undesirable class of persons, not often frankly
named in polite society. But the thing is by no
means so easy as it looks. The truth of history is
a very complex and very occult matter. It consists
of things which are invisible as well as of things
which are visible. It is full of secret motives, and
of a chance interplay of trivial and yet determining
circumstances; it is shot through with transient
passions, and broken athwart here and there by
what seem cruel accidents; it cannot all be reduced
to statistics or newspaper items or official recorded
statements. And so it turns out, when the actual
test of experiment is made, that the historian must

have something more than a good conscience, must be something more than a good man. He must have an eye to see the truth; and nothing but a very catholic imagination will serve to illuminate his matter for him: nothing less than keen and steady insight will make even illumination yield him the truth of what he looks upon. Even when he has seen the truth, only half his work is done, and that not the more difficult half. He must then make others see it just as he does: only when he has done that has he told the truth. What an art of penetrative phrase and just selection must he have to take others into the light in which he stands! Their dullness, their ignorance, their pre-possessions, are to be overcome and driven in, like a routed troop, upon the truth. The thing is infinitely difficult. The skill and strategy of it cannot be taught. And so historians take another way, which is easier: they tell part of the truth, — the part most to their taste, or most suitable to their talents, — and obtain readers to their liking among those of similar tastes and talents to their own.

We have our individual preferences in history, as in every other sort of literature. And there are histories to every taste: histories full of the piquant details of personal biography, histories that blaze with the splendors of courts and resound with drum and trumpet, and histories that run upon the humbler but greater levels of the life of the people; colorless histories, so passionless and so lacking in distinctive mark or motive that they might have been set up out of a dictionary without the intervention of an author, and partisan histories, so warped and violent in every judgment that no reader not of the historian's own party can stomach them; histories of economic development, and histories that speak only of politics; those that tell nothing but what it is pleasant and interesting to know, and those that tell nothing at all that one cares to remember. One must be of a new and unheard-of taste not to be suited among them all.

The trouble is, after all, that men do not invariably find the truth to their taste, and will often deny it when they hear it; and the historian has to do much more than keep his own eyes clear: he has also to catch and hold the eye of his reader. 'T is a nice art, as much intellectual as moral. How shall he take the palate of his reader at unawares, and get the unpalatable facts down his throat along with the palatable? Is there no way in which all the truth may be made to hold together in a narrative so strongly knit and so harmoniously colored that no reader will have either the wish or the skill to tear its patterns asunder, and men will take it all, unmarred and as it stands, rather than miss the zest of it?

It is evident the thing cannot be done by the " dispassionate " annalist. The old chroniclers, whom we relish, were not dispassionate. We love some of them for their sweet quaintness, some for their childlike credulity, some for their delicious inconsequentiality. But our modern chroniclers are not so. They are, above all things else, know-ing, thoroughly informed, subtly sophisticated. They would not for the world contribute any spice of their own to the narrative; and they are much too watchful, circumspect, and dutiful in their care to keep their method pure and untouched by any thought of theirs to let us catch so much as a glimpse of the chronicler underneath the chronicle. Their purpose is to give simply the facts, eschewing art, and substituting a sort of monumental index and table of the world's events.

The trouble is that men refuse to be made any wiser by such means. Though they will readily enough let their eyes linger upon a monument of art, they will heedlessly pass by a mere monument of industry. It suggests nothing to them. The materials may be suitable enough, but the handling of them leaves them dead and commonplace. An interesting circumstance thus comes to light. It is nothing less than this, that the facts do not of themselves constitute the truth. The truth is abstract, not concrete. It is the just idea, the right revelation of what things mean. It is evoked only by such arrangements and orderings of facts as suggest interpretations. The chronological arrangement of events, for example, may or may not be the arrangement which most surely brings the truth of the narrative to light ; and the best arrangement is always that which displays, not the facts themselves, but the subtle and else invisible forces that lurk in the events and in the minds of men, — forces for which events serve only as lasting and dramatic words of utterance. Take an instance. How are you to enable men to know the truth with regard to a period of revolution ? Will you give them simply a calm statement of recorded events, simply a quiet, unaccentuated narrative of what actually happened, written in a monotone, and verified by quotations from authentic documents of the time? You may save yourself the trouble. As well make a pencil sketch in outline of a raging conflagration ; write upon one portion of it "flame," upon another "smoke;" here "town hall, where the fire started," and there "spot where fireman was killed." It is a chart, not a picture. Even if you made a veritable picture of it, you could give only part of the truth so long as you confined yourself to black and white. Where would be all the wild and terrible colors of the scene : the red and tawny flame ; the masses of smoke, carrying the dull glare of the fire to the very skies, like a great signal banner thrown to the winds ; the hot and frightened faces of the crowd ; the crimsoned gables down the street, with the faint light of a lamp here and there gleaming white from some hastily opened casement ? Without the colors your picture is not true. No inventory of items will even represent the truth : the fuller and more minute you make your inventory, the more will the truth be obscured. The little details will take up as much space in the statement as the great totals into which they are summed up ; and, the proportions being false, the whole is false. Truth, fortunately, takes its own revenge. No one is deceived. The reader of the chronicle lays it aside. It lacks verisimilitude. He cannot realize how any of the things spoken of can have happened. He goes elsewhere to find, if he may, a real picture of the time, and perhaps finds one that is wholly fictitious. No wonder the grave and monk-like chronicler sighs. He of course wrote to be read, and not merely for the manual exercise of it ; and when he sees readers turn away his heart misgives him for his fellow-men. Is it as it always was, that they do not wish to know the truth? Alas! good eremite, men do not seek the truth as they should; but do you know what the truth is? It is a thing ideal, displayed by the just proportion of events, revealed in form and color, dumb till facts be set in syllables, articulated into words, put together into sentences, swung with proper tone and cadence. It is not revolutions only that have color. Nothing in human life is without it. In a monochrome you can depict nothing but a single incident; in a monotone you cannot often carry truth beyond a single sentence. Only by art in all its variety can you depict as it is the various face of life.

Yes; but what sort of art? There is here a wide field of choice. Shall we go back to the art of which Macaulay was so great a master? We could do worse. It must be a great art that can make men lay aside the novel and take up the history, to find there, in very fact, the movement and drama of life. What Macaulay does well he does incomparably. Who else can mass the details as he does, and yet not mar or obscure, but only heighten, the effect of the picture as a whole? Who else can bring so amazing a profusion of knowledge within the strait limits of a simple plan,

nowhere encumbered, everywhere free and obvious
in its movement? How sure the strokes, and how
bold and vivid the result! Yet when we have laid
the book aside, when the charm and the excitement
of the telling narrative have worn off, when we
have lost step with the swinging gait at which the
style goes, when the details have faded from our
recollection, and we sit removed and thoughtful,
with only the greater outlines of the story sharp
upon our minds, a deep misgiving and dissatisfaction take possession of us. We are no longer
young, and we are chagrined that we should have
been so pleased and taken with the glitter and
color and mere life of the picture. Let boys be
cajoled by rhetoric, we cry; men must look deeper.
What of the judgment of this facile and eloquent
man? Can we agree with him, when he is not
talking and the charm is gone? What shall we
say of his assessment of men and measures? Is
he just? Is he himself in possession of the whole
truth? Does he open the matter to us as it was?
Does he not, rather, rule us like an advocate, and
make himself master of our judgments?

Then it is that we become aware that there were
two Macaulays: Macaulay the artist, with an exquisite gift for telling a story, filling his pages with
little vignettes it is impossible to forget, fixing

these with an inimitable art upon the surface of a narrative that did not need the ornament they gave it, so strong and large and adequate was it; and Macaulay the Whig, subtly turning narrative into argument, and making history the vindication of a party. The mighty narrative is a great engine of proof. It is not told for its own sake. It is evidence summed up in order to justify a judgment. We detect the tone of the advocate, and though if we are just we must deem him honest, we cannot deem him safe. The great story-teller is discredited; and, willingly or unwillingly, we reject the guide who takes it upon himself to determine for us what we shall see. That, we feel sure, cannot be true which makes of so complex a history so simple a thesis for the judgment. There is art here; but it is the art of special pleading, misleading even to the pleader.

If not Macaulay, what master shall we follow? Shall our historian not have his convictions, and enforce them? Shall he not be our guide, and speak, if he can, to our spirits as well as to our understandings? Readers are a poor jury. They need enlightenment as well as information; the matter must be interpreted to them as well as related. There are moral facts as well as material, and the one sort must be as plainly told as the other. Of what service is it that the historian should have insight if we are not to know how the matter stands in his view? If he refrain from judgment, he may deceive us as much as he would were his judgment wrong; for we must have enlightenment, — that is his function. We would not set him up merely to tell us tales, but also to display to us characters, to open to us the moral and intent of the matter. Were the men sincere? Was the policy righteous? We have but just now seen that the " facts " lie deeper than the mere visible things that took place, that they involve the moral and motive of the play. Shall not these, too, be brought to light?

Unquestionably every sentence of true history must hold a judgment in solution. All cannot be told. If it were possible to tell all, it would take as long to write history as to enact it, and we should have to postpone the reading of it to the leisure of the next world. A few facts must be selected for the narrative, the great majority left unnoted. But the selection — for what purpose it is to be made? For the purpose of conveying *an impression* of the truth. Where shall you find a more radical process of judgment? The "essential" facts taken, the " unessential " left out! Why, you may make the picture what you will, and in any case it must

be the express image of the historian's fundamental
judgments. It is his purpose, or should be, to give
a true impression of his theme as a whole, — to
show it, not lying upon his page in an open and
dispersed analysis, but set close in intimate syn-
thesis, every line, every stroke, every bulk even,
omitted which does not enter of very necessity into
a single and unified image of the truth.

It is in this that the writing of history differs,
and differs very radically, from the statement of
the results of original research. The writing of
history must be based upon original research and
authentic record, but it can no more be directly
constructed by the piecing together of bits of
original research than by the mere reprinting together of state documents. Individual research
furnishes us, as it were, with the private documents
and intimate records without which the public
archives are incomplete and unintelligible. But
by themselves these are wholly out of perspective.
It is the consolation of those who produce them to
make them so. They would lose heart were they
forbidden to regard all facts as of equal importance.
It is facts they are after, and only facts, — facts
for their own sake, and without regard to their
several importance. These are their ore, — very
precious ore, — which they are concerned to get

out, not to refine. They have no direct concern with what may afterwards be done at the mint or in the goldsmith's shop. They will even boast that they care not for the beauty of the ore, and are indifferent how, or in what shape, it may become an article of commerce. Much of it is thrown away in the nice processes of manufacture, and you shall not distinguish the product of the several mines in the coin, or the cup, or the salver.

The historian must, indeed, himself be an investigator. He must know good ore from bad ; must distinguish fineness, quality, genuineness ; must stop to get out of the records for himself what he lacks for the perfection of his work. But for all that, he must know and stand ready to do every part of his task like a master workman, recognizing and testing every bit of stuff he uses. Standing sure, a man of science as well as an artist, he must take and use all of his equipment for the sake of his art, — not to display his materials, but to subordinate and transform them in his effort to make, by every touch and cunning of hand and tool, the perfect image of what he sees, the very truth of his seer's vision of the world. The true historian works always for the whole impression, the truth with unmarred proportions, unexaggerated parts, undistorted visage. He has no favorite parts of the story which he boasts are bits of his own, but loves only the whole of it, the full and unspoiled image of the day of which he writes, the crowded and yet consistent details which carry, without obtrusion of themselves, the large features of the time. Any exaggeration of the parts makes all the picture false, and the work is to do over. "Test every bit of material," runs the artist's rule, "and then forget the material;" forget its origin and the dross from which it has been freed, and think only and always of the great thing you would make of it, the pattern and form in which you would lose and merge it. That is its only high use.

'T is a pity to see how even the greatest minds will often lack the broad and catholic vision with which the just historian must look upon men and affairs. There is Carlyle, with his shrewd and seeing eye, his unmatched capacity to assess strong men and set the scenery for tragedy or intrigue, his breathless ardor for great events, his amazing flashes of insight, and his unlooked-for steady light of occasional narrative. The whole matter of what he writes is too dramatic. Surely history was not all enacted so hotly, or with so passionate a rush of men upon the stage. Its quiet scenes must have been longer, not mere pauses and interludes while the tragic parts were being made up. There is not often ordinary sunlight upon the page. The lights burn now wan, now lurid. Men are seen disquieted and turbulent, and may be heard in husky cries or rude, untimely jests. We do not recognize our own world, but seem to see another such as ours might become if peopled by like uneasy Titans. Incomparable to tell of days of storm and revolution, speaking like an oracle and familiar of destiny and fate, searching the hearts of statesmen and conquerors with an easy insight in every day of action, this peasant seer cannot give us the note of piping times of peace, or catch the tone of slow industry ; watches ships come and go at the docks, hears freight-vans thunder along the iron highways of the modern world, and loaded trucks lumber heavily through the crowded city streets, with a hot disdain of commerce, prices current, the haggling of the market, the smug ease of material comfort bred in a trading age. There is here no broad and catholic vision, no wise tolerance, no various power to know, to sympathize, to interpret. The great seeing imagination of the man lacks that pure radiance in which things are seen steadily and seen whole.

It is not easy, to say truth, to find actual examples when you are constructing the ideal historian,

the man with the vision and the faculty divine
to see affairs justly and tell of them completely.
If you are not satisfied with this passionate and
intolerant seer of Chelsea, whom will you choose?
Shall it be Gibbon, whom all praise, but so few
read? He, at any rate, is passionless, it would
appear. But who could write epochal history
with passion? All hot humors of the mind must,
assuredly, cool when spread at large upon so vast
a surface. One must feel like a sort of minor
providence in traversing that great tract of world
history, and catch in spite of one's self the gait and
manner of a god. This stately procession of generations moves on remote from the ordinary levels of
our human sympathy. 'T is a wide view of nations
and peoples and dynasties, and a world shaken by
the travail of new births. There is here no scale
by which to measure the historian of the sort we
must look to see handle the ordinary matter of
national history. The " Decline and Fall " stands
impersonal, like a monument. We shall reverence
it, but we shall not imitate it.

If we look away from Gibbon, exclude Carlyle,
and question Macaulay ; if we put the investigators
on one side as not yet historians, and the deliberately picturesque and entertaining *raconteurs* as
not yet investigators, we naturally turn, I suppose,

to such a man as John Richard Green, at once the patient scholar, — who shall adequately say how nobly patient? — and the rare artist, working so like a master in the difficult stuffs of a long national history. The very life of the man is as beautiful as the moving sentences he wrote with so subtle a music in the cadence. We know whence the fine moral elevation of tone came that sounds through all the text of his great narrative. True, not everybody is satisfied with our *doctor angelicus.* Some doubt he is too ornate. Others are troubled that he should sometimes be inaccurate. Some are willing to use his history as a manual; while others cannot deem him satisfactory for didactic uses, hesitate how they shall characterize him, and quit the matter vaguely with saying that what he wrote is "at any rate literature." Can there be something lacking in Green, too, notwithstanding he was impartial, and looked with purged and open eyes upon the whole unbroken life of his people, — notwithstanding he saw the truth and had the art and mastery to make others see it as he did, in all its breadth and multiplicity?

Perhaps even this great master of narrative lacks variety — as who does not? His method, whatever the topic, is ever the same. His sentences, his paragraphs, his chapters are pitched one and all in the same key. It is a very fine and moving key. Many an elevated strain and rich harmony commend it alike to the ear and to the imagination. It is employed with an easy mastery, and is made to serve to admiration a wide range of themes. But it is always the same key, and some themes it will not serve. An infinite variety plays through all history. Every scene has its own air and singularity. Incidents cannot all be rightly set in the narrative if all be set alike. As the scene shifts, the tone of the narrative must change : the narrator's choice of incident and his choice of words ; the speed and method of his sentence ; his own thought, even, and point of view. Surely his battle pages must resound with the tramp of armies and the fearful din and rush of war. In peace he must catch by turns the hum of industry, the bustle of the street, the calm of the country-side, the tone of parliamentary debate, the fancy, the ardor, the argument of poets and seers and quiet students. Snatches of song run along with sober-purpose and strenuous endeavor through every nation's story. Coarse men and refined, mobs and ordered assemblies, science and mad impulse, storm and calm, are all alike ingredients of the various life. It is not all epic. There is rough comedy and brutal violence. The drama can scarce be given any strict, unbroken harmony of incident, any close logical sequence of act or nice unity of scene.   To pitch it all in one key, therefore, is to mistake the significance of the infinite play of varied circumstance that makes up the yearly movement of a people's life.

It would be less than just to say that Green's pages do not reveal the variety of English life the centuries through.   It is his glory, indeed, as all the world knows, to have broadened and diversified the whole scale of English history.   Nowhere else within the compass of a single book can one find so many sides of the great English story displayed with so deep and just an appreciation of them all, or of the part of each in making up the whole. Green is the one man among English historians who has restored the great fabric of the nation's history where its architecture was obscure, and its details were likely to be lost or forgotten.   Once more, because of him, the vast Gothic structure stands complete, its majesty and firm grace enhanced at every point by the fine tracery of its restored details.

Where so much is done, it is no doubt unreasonable to ask for more.   But the very architectural symmetry of this great book imposes a limitation upon it.   It is full of a certain sort of variety; but it is only the variety of a great plan's detail, not the variety of English life. The noble structure obeys its own laws rather than the laws of a people's fortunes. It is a monument conceived and reared by a consummate artist, and it wears upon its every line some part of the image it was meant to bear, of a great, complex, aspiring national existence. But, though it symbolizes, it does not contain that life. It has none of the irregularity of the actual experiences of men and communities. It explains, but it does not contain, their variety. The history of every nation has certainly a plan which the historian must see and reproduce; but he must reconstruct the people's life, not merely expound it. The scope of his method must be as great as the variety of his subject; it must change with each change of mood, respond to each varying impulse in the great process of events. No rigor of a stately style must be suffered to exclude the lively touches of humor or the rude sallies of strength that mark it everywhere. The plan of the telling must answer to the plan of the fact, — must be as elastic as the topics are mobile. The matter should rule the plan, not the plan the matter.

The ideal is infinitely difficult, if, indeed, it be possible to any man not Shakespearean; but the

difficulty of attaining it is often unnecessarily enhanced. Ordinarily the historian's preparation for
his task is such as to make it unlikely he will
perform it naturally. He goes first, with infinite
and admirable labor, through all the labyrinth of
document and detail that lies up and down his
subject; collects masses of matter great and small,
for substance, verification, illustration; piles his
notes volumes high; reads far and wide upon the
tracks of his matter, and makes page upon page
of references; and then, thoroughly stuffed and
sophisticated, turns back and begins his narrative.
'T is impossible then that he should begin naturally.
He sees the end from the beginning, and all the in-
termediate way from beginning to end; he has made
up his mind about too many things; uses his details
with a too free and familiar mastery, not like one
who tells a story so much as like one who dissects a
cadaver. Having swept his details together beforehand, like so much scientific material, he discourses
upon them like a demonstrator, — thinks too little
in subjection to them. They no longer make a
fresh impression upon him. They are his tools,
not his objects of vision.

It is not by such a process that a narrative is
made vital and true. It does not do to lose the
point of view of the first listener to the tale, or to

rearrange the matter too much out of the order of nature. You must instruct your reader as the events themselves would have instructed him, had he been able to note them as they passed. The historian must not lose his own fresh view of the scene as it passed and changed more and more from year to year and from age to age. He must keep with the generation of which he writes, not be too quick to be wiser than they were or look back upon them in his narrative with head over shoulder. He must write of them always in the atmosphere they themselves breathed, not hastening to judge them, but striving only to realize them at every turn of the story, to make their thoughts his own, and call their lives back again, rebuilding the very stage upon which they played their parts. Bring the end of your story to mind while you set about telling its beginning, and it seems to have no parts: beginning, middle, end, are all as one, — are merely like parts of a pattern which you see as a single thing stamped upon the stuff under your hand.

Try the method with the history of our own land and people. How will you begin? Will you start with a modern map and a careful topographical description of the continent? And then, having made your nineteenth-century framework for the narrative, will you ask your reader to turn back and see the seventeenth century, and those lonely ships coming in at the capes of the Chesapeake ? He will never see them so long as you compel him to stand here at the end of the nineteenth century and look at them as if through a long retrospect. The attention both of the narrator and of the reader, if history is to be seen aright, must look forward, not backward. It must see with a contemporaneous eye. Let the historian, if he be wise, know no more of the history as he writes than might have been known in the age and day of which he is writing. A trifle too much knowledge will undo him. It will break the spell for his imagination. It will spoil the magic by which he may raise again the image of days that are gone. He must of course know the large lines of his story ; it must lie as a whole in his mind. His very art demands that, in order that he may know and keep its proportions. But the details, the passing incidents of day and year, must come fresh into his mind, unreasoned upon as yet, untouched by theory, with their first look upon them. It is here that original documents and fresh research will serve him. He must look far and wide upon every detail of the time, see it at first hand, and paint as he looks ; selecting, as the artist must, but selecting while the vision is fresh, and not from old sketches laid away in his notes, — selecting from the life itself.

Let him remember that his task is radically different from the task of the investigator. The investigator must display his materials, but the historian must convey his impressions. He must stand in the presence of life, and reproduce it in his narrative; must recover a past age; make dead generations live again and breathe their own air; show them native and at home upon his page. To do this, his own impressions must be as fresh as those of an unlearned reader, his own curiosity as keen and young at every stage. It may easily be so as his reading thickens, and the atmosphere of the age comes stealthily into his thought, if only he take care to push forward the actual writing of his narrative at an equal pace with his reading, painting thus always direct from the image itself. His knowledge of the great outlines and bulks of the picture will be his sufficient guide and restraint the while, will give proportion to the individual strokes of his work. But it will not check his zest, or sophisticate his fresh recovery of the life that is in the crowding colors of the canvas.

A nineteenth-century plan laid like a standard and measure upon a seventeenth-century narrative will infallibly twist it and make it false. Lay a modern map before the first settlers at Jamestown and Plymouth, and then bid them discover and occupy the continent. With how superior a nineteenth-century wonder and pity will you see them grope, and stumble, and falter! How like children they will seem to you, and how simple their age, and ignorant! As stalwart men as you they were in fact; mayhap wiser and braver too; as fit to occupy a continent as you are to draw it upon paper. If you would know them, go back to their age; breed yourself a pioneer and woodsman; look to find the South Sea up the nearest northwest branch of the spreading river at your feet; discover and occupy the wilderness with them; dream what may be beyond the near hills, and long all day to see a sail upon the silent sea; go back to them and see them in their habit as they lived.

The picturesque writers of history have all along been right in theory: they have been wrong only in practice. It *is* a picture of the past we want — its express image and feature; but we want the true picture and not simply the theatrical matter, — the manner of Rembrandt rather than of Rubens. All life may be pictured, but not all of life is picturesque. No great, no true historian would put false or adventitious colors into his narrative, or let a glamour rest where in fact it never was. The writers who select an incident merely because it is striking or dramatic are shallow fellows. They see only with the eye's retina, not with that deep vision whose images lie where thought and reason sit. The real drama of life is disclosed only with the whole picture; and that only the deep and fervid student will see, whose mind goes daily fresh to the details, whose narrative runs always in the authentic colors of nature, whose art it is to see, and to paint what he sees.

It is thus and only thus we shall have the truth of the matter: by art, — by the most difficult of all arts; by fresh study and first-hand vision; at the mouths of men who stand in the midst of old letters and dusty documents and neglected records, not like antiquarians, but like those who see a distant country and a far-away people before their very eyes, as real, as full of life and hope and incident, as the day in which they themselves live. Let us have done with humbug and come to plain speech. The historian needs an imagination quite as much as he needs scholarship, and consummate literary art as much as candor and common honesty. Histories are written in order that the bulk of men may read and realize; and it is as bad to bungle the telling of the story as to lie, as fatal to lack a vocabulary as to lack knowledge. In no case can you do more than convey an impression, so various and complex is the matter. If you convey a false impression, what difference does it make how you convey it? In the whole process there is a nice adjustment of means to ends which only the artist can manage. There is an art of lying; — there is equally an art, — an infinitely more difficult art, — of telling the truth.

VII.

BEFORE a calendar of great Americans can be made out, a valid canon of Americanism must first be established. Not every great man born and bred in America was a great " American." Some of the notable men born among us were simply great Englishmen ; others had in all the habits of their thought and life the strong flavor of a peculiar region, and were great New Englanders or great Southerners ; others, masters in the fields of science or of pure thought, showed nothing either distinctively national or characteristically provincial, and were simply great men ; while a few displayed odd cross-strains of blood or breeding. The great Englishmen bred in America, like Hamilton and Madison ; the great provincials, like John Adams and Calhoun ; the authors of such thought as might have been native to any clime, like Asa Gray and Emerson ; and the men of mixed breed, like Jefferson and Benton, — must be excluded from our present list. We must pick out men who have created or exemplified a distinctively American standard and type of greatness.

To make such a selection is not to create an artificial standard of greatness, or to claim that greatness is in any case hallowed or exalted merely because it is American. It is simply to recognize a peculiar stamp of character, a special make-up of mind and faculties, as the specific product of our national life, not displacing or eclipsing talents of a different kind, but supplementing them, and so adding to the world's variety. There is an American type of man, and those who have exhibited this type with a certain unmistakable distinction and perfection have been great "Americans." It has required the utmost variety of character and energy to establish a great nation, with a polity at once free and firm, upon this continent, and no sound type of manliness could have been dispensed with in the effort. We could no more have done without our great Englishmen, to keep the past steadily in mind and make every change conservative of principle, than we could have done without the men whose whole impulse was forward, whose whole genius was for origination, natural masters of the art of subduing a wilderness.

Certainly one of the greatest figures in our history is the figure of Alexander Hamilton. American historians, though compelled always to admire him, often in spite of themselves, have been inclined, like the mass of men in his own day, to look at him askance. They hint, when they do not plainly say, that he was not " American." He rejected, if he did not despise, democratic principles; advocated a government as strong, almost, as a monarchy; and defended the government which was actually set up, like the skilled advocate he was, only because it was the strongest that could be had under the circumstances. He believed in authority, and he had no faith in the aggregate wisdom of masses of men. He had, it is true, that deep and passionate love of liberty, and that steadfast purpose in the maintenance of it, that mark the best Englishmen everywhere; but his ideas of government stuck fast in the old-world politics, and his statesmanship was of Europe rather than of America. And yet the genius and the steadfast spirit of this man were absolutely indispensable to us. No one less masterful, no one less resolute than he to drill the minority, if necessary, to have their way against the majority, could have done the great work of organization by which he established the national credit, and with the national credit the national government itself. A pliant, popular, optimistic man would have failed utterly in the task. A great radical mind in his place would have brought disaster upon us : only a great conservative genius could have succeeded. It is safe to say that, without men of Hamilton's cast of mind, building the past into the future with a deep passion for order and old wisdom, our national life would have miscarried at the very first. This tried English talent for conservation gave to our fibre at the very outset the stiffness of maturity.

James Madison, too, we may be said to have inherited. His invaluable gifts of counsel were of the sort so happily imparted to us with our English blood at the first planting of the States which formed the Union. A grave and prudent man, and yet brave withal when new counsel was to be taken, he stands at the beginning of our national history, even in his young manhood, as he faced and led the constitutional convention, a type of the slow and thoughtful English genius for affairs. He held old and tested convictions of the uses of liberty ; he was competently read in the history of government ; processes of revolution were in his thought no more than processes of adaptation : exigencies were to be met by modification, not by experiment. His reasonable spirit runs through all the proceedings of the great convention that gave us the Constitution, and that noble instrument seems the product of character like his. For all it is so American in its content, it is in its method a thoroughly English production, so full is it of old principles, so conservative of experience, so carefully compounded of compromises, of concessions made and accepted. Such men are of a stock so fine as to need no titles to make it noble, and yet so old and so distinguished as actually to bear the chief titles of English liberty. Madison came of the long line of English constitutional statesmen.

There is a type of genius which closely approaches this in character, but which is, nevertheless, distinctively American. It is to be seen in John Marshall and in Daniel Webster. In these men a new set of ideas find expression, ideas which all the world has received as American. Webster was not an English but an American constitutional statesman. For the English statesman constitutional issues are issues of policy rather than issues of law. He constantly handles questions of change: his constitution is always a-making. He must at every turn construct, and he is deemed conservative if only his rule be consistency and continuity with the past. He will search diligently for precedent, but he is content if the precedent contain only a germ of the policy he proposes. His standards are set him, not by law, but by opinion: his constitution is an ideal of cautious and orderly change. Its fixed element is the conception of political liberty: a conception which, though steeped in history, must ever be added to and altered by social change. The American constitutional statesman, on the contrary, constructs policies like a lawyer. The standard with which he must square his conduct is set him by a document upon whose definite sentences the whole structure of the government directly rests. That document, moreover, is the concrete embodiment of a peculiar theory of government. That theory is, that definitive laws, selected by a power outside the government, are the structural iron of the entire fabric of politics, and that nothing which cannot be constructed upon this stiff framework is a safe or legitimate part of policy. Law is, in his conception, creative of states, and they live only by such permissions as they can extract from it. The functions of the judge and the functions of the man of affairs have, therefore, been very closely related in our history, and John Marshall, scarcely less than Daniel Webster, was a constitutional statesman. With all Madison's conservative temper and wide-eyed prudence in counsel, the subject-matter of thought for both of these men was not English liberty or the experience of men everywhere in self-govern-

ment, but the meaning stored up in the explicit
sentences of a written fundamental law. They
taught men the new — the American — art of
extracting life out of the letter, not of statutes
merely (that art was not new), but of statute-built
institutions and documented governments : the art
of saturating politics with law without grossly dis-
coloring law with politics. Other nations have
had written constitutions, but no other nation has
ever filled a written constitution with this singularly
compounded content, of a sound legal conscience
and a strong national purpose. It would have
been easy to deal with our Constitution like subtle
dialecticians ; but Webster and Marshall did much
more and much better than that. They viewed
the fundamental law as a great organic product, a
vehicle of life as well as a charter of authority ; in
disclosing its life they did not damage its tissue ;
and in thus expanding the law without impairing
its structure or authority they made great contributions alike to statesmanship and to jurisprudence.
Our notable literature of decision and commentary
in the field of constitutional law is America's
distinctive 'gift to the history and the science of
law. John Marshall wrought out much of its substance ; Webster diffused its great body of principles throughout national policy, mediating between

the law and affairs.   The figures of the two men must hold the eye of the world as the figures of two great national representatives, as the figures of two great Americans.

The representative national greatness and function of these men appear more clearly still when they are contrasted with men like John Adams and John C. Calhoun, whose greatness was not national.   John Adams represented one element of our national character, and represented it nobly, with a singular force and greatness.   He was an eminent Puritan statesman, and the Puritan ingredient has colored all our national life.   We have got strength and persistency and some part of our steady moral purpose from it.   But in the quick growth and exuberant expansion of the nation it has been only one element among many.   The Puritan blood has mixed with many another strain.   The stiff Puritan character has been mellowed by many a transfusion of gentler and more hopeful elements.   So soon as the Adams fashion of man became more narrow, intense, acidulous, intractable, according to the tendencies of its nature, in the person of John Quincy Adams, it lost the sympathy, lost even the tolerance, of the country, and the national choice took its reckless leap from a Puritan President to Andrew Jackson, a man cast in the rough original pattern of American life at the heart of the continent. John Adams had not himself been a very acceptable President. He had none of the national optimism, and could not understand those who did have it. He had none of the characteristic adaptability of the delocalized American, and was just a bit ridiculous in his stiffness at the Court of St. James, for all he was so honorable and so imposing. His type, — be it said without disrespect, — was provincial. Unmistakably a great man, his greatness was of the commonwealth, not of the empire.

Calhoun, too, was a great provincial. Although a giant, he had no heart to use his great strength for national purposes. In his youth, it is true, he did catch some of the generous ardor for national enterprise which filled the air in his day; and all his life through, with a truly pathetic earnestness, he retained his affection for his first ideal. But when the rights and interests of his section were made to appear incompatible with a liberal and boldly constructive interpretation of the Constitution, he fell out of national counsels and devoted all the strength of his extraordinary mind to holding the nation's thought and power back within the strait limits of a literal construction of the law. In powers of reasoning his mind deserves to rank with Webster's and Marshall's : he handled questions of law like a master, as they did. He had, moreover, a keen insight into the essential principles and character of liberty. IIis thought moved eloquently along some of the oldest and safest lines of English thought in the field of government. He made substantive contributions to the permanent philosophy of politics. His reasoning has been discredited, not so much because it was not theoretically sound within its limits, as because its practical outcome was a negation which embarrassed the whole movement of national affairs. He would have held the nation still, in an old equipoise, at one time normal enough, but impossible to maintain. Webster and Marshall gave leave to the energy of change inherent in all the national life, making law a rule, but not an interdict ; a living guide, but not a blind and rigid discipline. Calhoun sought to fix, law as a barrier across the path of policy, commanding the life of the nation to stand still. The strength displayed in the effort, the intellectual power and address, abundantly entitle him to be called great ; but his purpose was not national. It regarded only a section of the country, and marked him, — again be it said with all respect, — a great provincial.

Jefferson was not a thorough American because

of the strain of French philosophy that permeated and weakened all his thought. Benton was altogether American so far as the natural strain of his blood was concerned, but he had encumbered his natural parts and inclinations with a mass of undigested and shapeless learning. Bred in the West, where everything was new, he had filled his head with the thought of books (evidently very poor books) which exhibited the ideals of communities in which everything was old. He thought of the Roman Senate when he sat in the Senate of the United States. He paraded classical figures whenever he spoke, upon a stage where both their costume and their action seemed grotesque. A pedantic frontiersman, he was a living and a pompous antinomy. Meant by nature to be an American, he spoiled the plan by applying a most unsuitable gloss of shallow and irrelevant learning. Jefferson was of course an almost immeasurably greater man than Benton, but he was un-American in somewhat the same way. He brought a foreign product of thought to a market where no natural or wholesome demand for it could exist. There were not two incompatible parts in him, as in Benton's case: he was a philosophical radical by nature as well as by acquirement; his reading and his temperament went suitably together. The man is

homogeneous throughout. The American shows in
him very plainly, too, notwithstanding the strong
and inherent dash of what was foreign in his
make-up. He was a natural leader and manager
of men, not because he was imperative or masterful, but because of a native shrewdness, tact, and
sagacity, an inborn art and aptness for combination,
such as no Frenchman ever displayed in the management of common men. Jefferson had just a
touch of rusticity about him, besides ; and it was
not pretense on his part or merely a love of power
that made him democratic. His indiscriminate
hospitality, his almost passionate love for the simple equality of country life, his steady devotion to
what he deemed to be the cause of the people, all
mark him a genuine democrat, a nature native to
America. It is his speculative philosophy that is
exotic, and that runs like a false and artificial note
through all his thought. It was un-American in
being abstract, sentimental, rationalistic, rather
than practical. That he held it sincerely need not
be doubted ; but the more sincerely he accepted it
so much the more thoroughly was he un-American.
His writings lack hard and practical sense. Liberty, among us, is not a sentiment, but a product
of experience; its derivation is not rationalistic,
but practical. It is a hard-headed spirit of inde-

pendence, not the conclusion of a syllogism. The very aërated quality of Jefferson's principles gives them an air of insincerity, which attaches to them rather because they do not suit the climate of the country and the practical aspect of affairs than because they do not suit the character of Jefferson's mind and the atmosphere of abstract philosophy. It is because both they and the philosophical system of which they form a part do seem suitable to his mind and character, that we must pronounce him, though a great man, not a great American.

It is by the frank consideration of such concrete cases that we may construct, both negatively and affirmatively, our canons of Americanism. The American spirit is something more than the old, the immemorial Saxon spirit of liberty from which it sprung. It has been bred by the conditions attending the great task which we have all the century been carrying forward: the task, at once material and ideal, of subduing a wilderness and covering all the wide stretches of a vast continent with a single free and stable polity. It is, accordingly, above all things, a hopeful and confident spirit. It is progressive, optimistically progressive, and ambitious of objects of national scope and advantage. It is unpedantic, unprovincial, unspeculative, unfastidious; regardful of law, but as using it, not as being used by it or dominated by any formalism whatever; in a sense unrefined, because full of rude force; but prompted by large and generous motives, and often as tolerant as it is resolute. No one man, unless it be Lincoln, has ever proved big or various enough to embody this active and full-hearted spirit in all its qualities; and the men who have been too narrow or too speculative or too pedantic to represent it have, nevertheless, added to the strong and stirring variety of our national life, making it fuller and richer in motive and energy; but its several aspects are none the less noteworthy as they separately appear in different men.

One of the first men to exhibit this American spirit with an unmistakable touch of greatness and distinction was Benjamin Franklin. It was characteristic of America that this self-made man should become a philosopher, a founder of philosophical societies, an authoritative man of science; that his philosophy of life should be so homely and so practical in its maxims, and uttered with so shrewd a wit; that one region should be his birthplace and another his home; that he should favor effective political union among the colonies from the first, and should play a sage and active part in the establishment of national independence and the

planning of a national organization; and that he
should represent his countrymen in diplomacy
abroad. They could have had no spokesman who
represented more sides of their character. Franklin
was a sort of multiple American. He was versatile
without lacking solidity; he was a practical statesman without ceasing to be a sagacious philosopher.
He came of the people, and was democratic; but
he had raised himself out of the general mass of
unnamed men, and so stood for the democratic law,
not of equality, but of self-selection in endeavor.
One can feel sure that Franklin would have succeeded in any part of the national life that it might
have fallen to his lot to take part in. He will
stand the final and characteristic test of Americanism : he would unquestionably have made a successful frontiersman, capable at once of wielding the
axe and of administering justice from the fallen
trunk.

Washington hardly seems an American, as most
of his biographers depict him. He is too colorless,
too cold, too prudent. He seems more like a wise
and dispassionate Mr. Alworthy, advising a nation
as he would a parish, than like a man building
states and marshaling a nation in a wilderness.
But the real Washington was as thoroughly an
American as Jackson or Lincoln. What we take

for lack of passion in him was but the reserve and
self-mastery natural to a man of his class and
breeding in Virginia. He was no parlor politician,
either. He had seen the frontier, and far beyond
it where the French forts lay. He knew the rough
life of the country as few other men could. His
thoughts did not live at Mount Vernon. He knew
difficulty as intimately and faced it always with as
quiet a mastery as William the Silent. This calm,
straightforward, high-spirited man, making charts
of the western country, noting the natural land
and water routes into the heart of the continent,
marking how the French power lay, conceiving the
policy which should dispossess it, and the engineer-
ing achievements which should make the utmost
resources of the land our own; counseling Brad-
dock how to enter the forest, but not deserting him
because he would not take advice; planning step
by step, by patient correspondence with influential
men everywhere, the meetings, conferences, common resolves which were finally to bring the great
constitutional convention together; planning, too,
always for the country as well as for Virginia; and
presiding at last over the establishment and organization of the government of the Union: he certainly
— the most suitable instrument of the national life
at every moment of crisis — is a great American.

Those noble words which he uttered amidst the first doubtings of the constitutional convention might serve as a motto for the best efforts of liberty wherever free men strive: " Let us raise a standard to which the wise and honest can repair; the event is in the hand of God."

In Henry Clay we have an American of a most authentic pattern. There was no man of his generation who represented more of America than he did. The singular, almost irresistible attraction he had for men of every class and every temperament came, not from the arts of the politician, but from the instant sympathy established between him and every fellow-countryman of his. He does not seem to have exercised the same fascination upon foreigners. They felt toward him as some New Englanders did: he seemed to them plausible merely, too indiscriminately open and cordial to be sincere, — a bit of a charlatan. No man who really takes the trouble to understand Henry Clay, or who has quick enough parts to sympathize with him, can deem him false. It is the odd combination of two different elements in him that makes him seem irregular and inconstant. His nature was of the West, blown through with quick winds of ardor and aggression, a bit reckless and defiant; but his art was of the East, ready with soft and

placating phrases, reminiscent of old and reverenced
ideals, thoughtful of compromise and accommoda-
tion.   He had all the address of the trained and
sophisticated politician, bred in an old and sensitive
society; but his purposes ran free of cautious restraints, and his real ideals were those of the somewhat bumptious Americanism which was pushing
the frontier forward in the West, which believed
itself capable of doing anything it might put its
hand to, despised conventional restraints, and
followed a vague but resplendent " manifest destiny " with lusty hurrahs.   His purposes were sincere, even if often crude and uninstructed; it was
only because the subtle arts of politics seemed in-
consistent with the direct dash and bold spirit of
the man that they sat upon him like an insincerity.   He thoroughly, and by mere unconscious sympathy, represented the double America of his day,
made up of a West which hurried and gave bold
strokes, and of an East which held back, fearing
the pace, thoughtful and mindful of the instructive past.   The one part had to be served without
offending the other: and that was Clay's medi-
atorial function.

Andrew Jackson was altogether of the West.
Of his sincerity nobody has ever had any real
doubt; and his Americanism is now at any rate

equally unimpeachable. He was like Clay with
the social imagination of the orator and the art
and sophistication of the Eastern politician left out.
He came into our national politics like a cyclone
from off the Western prairies. Americans of the
present day perceptibly shudder at the very recollection of Jackson. He seems to them a great
Vandal, playing fast and loose alike with institutions and with tested and established policy, de-
bauching politics like a modern spoilsman. But
whether we would accept him as a type of ourselves
or not, the men of his own day accepted him with
enthusiasm. He did not need to be explained to
them. They crowded to his standard like men
free at last, after long and tedious restraint, to
make their own choice, follow their own man.
There can be no mistaking the spontaneity of the
thoroughgoing support he received. His was the
new type of energy and self-confidence bred by
life outside the States that had been colonies. It
was a terrible energy, threatening sheer destruction
to many a carefully wrought arrangement handed
on to us from the past ; it was a perilous self-confidence, founded in sheer strength rather than in
wisdom. The government did not pass through
the throes of that signal awakening of the new
national spirit without serious rack and damage.

But it was no disease.   It was only an incautious, abounding, madcap strength which proved so dangerous in its readiness for every rash endeavor.   It was necessary that the West should be let into the play : it was even necessary that she should assert her right to the leading rôle.   It was done without good taste, but that does not condemn it.   We have no doubt refined and schooled the hoyden influences of that crude time, and they are vastly safer now than then, when they first came bounding in ; but they mightily stirred and enriched our blood from the first.   Now that we have thoroughly suffered this Jackson change and it is over, we are ready to recognize it as quite as radically American as anything in all our history.

Lincoln, nevertheless, rather than Jackson, was the supreme American of our history.   In Clay, East and West were mixed without being fused or harmonized : he seems like two men.   In Jackson there was not even a mixture ; he was all of a piece, and altogether unacceptable to some parts of the country, — a frontier statesman.   But in Lincoln the elements were combined and harmonized.   The most singular thing about the wonderful career of the man is the way in which he steadily grew into a national stature.   He began an amorphous, unlicked cub, bred in the rudest of human lairs ;

but, as he grew, everything formed, informed, transformed him. The process was slow but unbroken. He was not fit to be President until he actually became President. He was fit then because, learning everything as he went, he had found out how much there was to learn, and had still an infinite capacity for learning. The quiet voices of sentiment and murmurs of resolution that went whispering through the land, his ear always caught, when others could hear nothing but their own words. He never ceased to be a common man : that was his source of strength. But he was a common man with genius, a genius for things American, for insight into the common thought, for mastery of the fundamental things of politics that inhere in human nature and cast hardly more than their shadows on constitutions ; for the practical niceties of affairs ; for judging men and assessing arguments. Jackson had no social imagination : no unfamiliar community made any impression on him. His whole fibre stiffened young, and nothing afterward could modify or even deeply affect it. But Lincoln was always a-making ; he would have died unfinished if the terrible storms of the war had not stung him to learn in those four years what no other twenty could have taught him. And, as he stands there in his complete manhood, at the most perilous helm in Christendom, what a marvelous composite figure he is! The whole country is summed up in him: the rude Western strength, tempered with shrewdness and a broad and humane wit; the Eastern conservatism, regardful of law and devoted to fixed standards of duty. He even understood the South, as no other Northern man of his generation did. He respected, because he comprehended, though he could not hold, its view of the Constitution; he appreciated the inexorable compulsions of its past in respect of slavery; he would have secured it once more, and speedily if possible, in its right to self-government, when the fight was fought out. To the Eastern politicians he seemed like an accident; but to history he must seem like a providence.

Grant was Lincoln's suitable instrument, a great American general, the appropriate product of West Point. A Western man, he had no thought of commonwealths politically separate, and was instinctively for the Union; a man of the common people, he deemed himself always an instrument, never a master, and did his work, though ruthlessly, without malice; a sturdy, hard-willed, taciturn man, a sort of Lincoln the Silent in thought and spirit. He does not appeal to the imagination very deeply; there is a sort of common greatness about him, great gifts combined singularly with a great mediocrity; but such peculiarities seem to make him all the more American, — national in spirit, thoroughgoing in method, masterful in purpose.

And yet it is no contradiction to say that Robert E. Lee also was a great American. He fought on the opposite side, but he fought in the same spirit, and for a principle which is in a sense scarcely less American than the principle of Union. He represented the idea of the inherent — the essential — separateness of self-government. This was not the principle of secession : that principle involved the separate right of the several self-governing units of the federal system to judge of national questions independently, and as a check upon the federal government, — to adjudge the very objects of the Union. Lee did not believe in secession, but he did believe in the local rootage of all government. This is at the bottom, no doubt, an English idea; but it has had a characteristic American development. It is the reverse side of the shield which bears upon its obverse the devices of the Union, a side too much overlooked and obscured since the war. It conceives the individual State a community united by the most intimate associations, the first home and foster-mother of every man born into the citizenship of the nation. Lee considered himself a member of one of these great families; he could not conceive of the nation apart from the State: above all, he could not live in the nation divorced from his neighbors. His own community should decide his political destiny and duty.

This was also the spirit of Patrick Henry and of Sam Houston, — men much alike in the cardinal principle of their natures. Patrick Henry resisted the formation of the Union only because he feared to disturb the local rootage of self-government, to disperse power so widely that neighbors could not control it. It was not a disloyal or a separatist spirit, but only a jealous spirit of liberty. Sam Houston, too, deemed the character a community should give itself so great a matter that the community, once made, ought itself to judge of the national associations most conducive to its liberty and progress. Without liberty of this intensive character there could have been no vital national liberty; and Sam Houston, Patrick Henry, and Robert E. Lee are none the less great Americans because they represented only one cardinal principle of the national life. Self-government has its intrinsic antinomies as well as its harmonies.

Among men of letters Lowell is doubtless most

typically American, though Curtis must find an eligible place in the list. Lowell was self-conscious, though the truest greatness is not; he was a trifle too " smart," besides, and there is no " smartness " in great literature. But both the self-consciousness and the smartness must be admitted to be American; and Lowell was so versatile, so urbane, of so large a spirit, and so admirable in the scope of his sympathies, that he must certainly go on the calendar.

There need be no fear that we shall be obliged to stop with Lowell in literature, or with any of the men who have been named in the field of achievement. We shall not in the future have to take one type of Americanism at a time. The frontier is gone: it has reached the Pacific. The country grows rapidly homogeneous. With the same pace it grows various, and multiform in all its life. The man of the simple or local type cannot any longer deal in the great manner with any national problem. The great men of our future must be of the composite type of greatness: sound-hearted, hopeful, confident of the validity of liberty, tenacious of the deeper principles of American institutions, but with the old rashness schooled and sobered, and instinct tempered by instruction. They must be wise with an adult, not with an adolescent wisdom. Some day we shall be of one mind, our ideals fixed, our purposes harmonized, our nationality complete and consentaneous: then will come our great literature and our greatest men.

VIII.

THE COURSE OF AMERICAN HISTORY.[1]

In the field of history, learning should be deemed to stand among the people and in the midst of life. Its function there is not one of pride merely: to make complaisant record of deeds honorably done and plans nobly executed in the past. It has also a function of guidance: to build high places whereon to plant the clear and flaming lights of experience, that they may shine alike upon the roads already traveled and upon the paths not yet attempted. The historian is also a sort of prophet. Our memories direct us. They give us knowledge of our character, alike in its strength and in its weakness: and it is so we get our standards for endeavor, — our warnings and our gleams of hope. It is thus we learn what manner of nation we are of, and divine what manner of people we should be.

And this is not in national records merely. Local history is the ultimate substance of national history. There could be no epics were pastorals

[1] An address delivered before the New Jersey Historical Society.

not also true, — no patriotism, were there no homes,
no neighbors, no quiet round of civic duty; and I,
for my part, do not wonder that scholarly men
have been found not a few who, though they might
have shone upon a larger field, where all eyes
would have seen them win their fame, yet chose
to pore all their lives long upon the blurred and
scattered records of a country-side, where there was
nothing but an old church or an ancient village.
The history of a nation is only the history of its
villages written large. I only marvel that these
local historians have not seen more in the stories
they have sought to tell. Surely here, in these old
hamlets that antedate the cities, in these little
communities that stand apart and yet give their
young life to the nation, is to be found the very
authentic stuff of romance for the mere looking.
There is love and courtship and eager life and
high devotion up and down all the lines of every
genealogy. What strength, too, and bold endeavor
in the cutting down of forests to make the clear-
ings; what breath of hope and discovery in scaling
for the first time the nearest mountains; what
longings ended or begun upon the coming in of
ships into the harbor; what pride of earth in the
rivalries of the village; what thoughts of heaven
in the quiet of the rural church! What forces of

slow and steadfast endeavor there were in the building of a great city upon the foundations of a hamlet : and how the plot broadens and thickens and grows dramatic as communities widen into states! Here, surely, sunk deep in the very fibre of the stuff, are the colors of the great story of men, — the lively touches of reality and the striking images of life.

It must be admitted, I know, that local history can be made deadly dull in the telling. The men who reconstruct it seem usually to build with kiln-dried stuff, — as if with a purpose it should last. But that is not the fault of the subject. National history may be written almost as ill, if due pains be taken to dry it out. It is a trifle more difficult: because merely to speak of national affairs is to give hint of great forces and of movements blown upon by all the airs of the wide continent. The mere largeness of the scale lends to the narrative a certain dignity and spirit. But some men will manage to be dull though they should speak of creation. In writing of local history the thing is fatally easy. For there is some neighborhood history that lacks any large significance, which is without horizon or outlook. There are details in the history of every community which it concerns no man to know again when once they are past

and decently buried in the records: and these are
the very details, no doubt, which it is easiest to
find upon a casual search. It is easier to make
out a list of county clerks than to extract the social
history of the county from the records they have
kept, — though it is not so important: and it is
easier to make a catalogue of anything than to say
what of life and purpose the catalogue stands for.
This is called collecting facts " for the sake of the
facts themselves; " but if I wished to do aught for
the sake of the facts themselves I think I should
serve them better by giving their true biographies
than by merely displaying their faces.

The right and vital sort of local history is the
sort which may be written with lifted eyes, — the
sort which has an horizon and an outlook upon
the world. Sometimes it may happen, indeed,
that the annals of a neighborhood disclose some
singular adventure which had its beginning and its
ending there: some unwonted bit of fortune which
stands unique and lonely amidst the myriad trans-
actions of the world of affairs, and deserves to be
told singly and for its own sake. But usually the
significance of local history is, that it is part of a
greater whole. A spot of local history is like an
inn upon a highway: it is a stage upon a far
journey: it is a place the national history has

passed through. There mankind has stopped and lodged by the way. Local history is thus less than national history only as the part is less than the whole. The whole could not dispense with the part, would not exist without it, could not be understood unless the part also were understood. Local history is subordinate to national only in the sense in which each leaf of a book is subordinate to the volume itself. Upon no single page will the whole theme of the book be found; but each page holds a part of the theme. Even were the history of each locality exactly like the history of every other (which it cannot be), it would deserve to be written, — if only to corroborate the history of the rest, and verify it as an authentic part of the record of the race and nation. The common elements of a nation's life are the great elements of its life, the warp and woof of the fabric. They cannot be too much or too substantially verified and explicated. It is so that history is made solid and fit for use and wear.

Our national history, of course, has its own great and spreading pattern, which can be seen in its full form and completeness only when the stuff of our national life is laid before us in broad surfaces and upon an ample scale. But the detail of the pattern, the individual threads of the great fabric,

are to be found only in local history. There is all
the intricate weaving, all the delicate shading, all
the nice refinement of the pattern, — gold thread
mixed with fustian, fine thread laid upon coarse,
shade combined with shade. Assuredly it is this
that gives to local history its life and importance.
The idea, moreover, furnishes a nice criterion of
interest.   The life of some localities is, obviously,
more completely and intimately a part of the
national pattern than the life of other localities,
which are more separate and, as it were, put upon
the border of the fabric. To come at once and
very candidly to examples, the local history of the
Middle States, — New York, New Jersey, and
Pennsylvania, — is much more structurally a part
of the characteristic life of the nation as a whole
than is the history of the New England communities
or of the several States and regions of the South.
I know that such a heresy will sound very rank in
the ears of some : for I am speaking against accepted doctrine. But acceptance, be it never so
general, does not make a doctrine true.

Our national history has been written for the
most part by New England men. All honor to
them ! Their scholarship and their characters alike
have given them an honorable enrollment amongst
the great names of our literary history ; and no

just man would say aught to detract, were it never
so little, from their well-earned fame. They have
written our history, nevertheless, from but a single
point of view. From where they sit, the whole of
the great development looks like an Expansion of
New England. Other elements but play along the
sides of the great process by which the Puritan has
worked out the development of nation and polity.
It is he who has gone out and possessed the land:
the man of destiny, the type and impersonation of
a chosen people. To the Southern writer, too, the
story looks much the same, if it be but followed to
its culmination, — to its final storm and stress and
tragedy in the great war. It is the history of the
Suppression of the South. Spite of all her splendid contributions to the steadfast accomplishment
of the great task of building the nation; spite of
the long leadership of her statesmen in the national
counsels; spite of her joint achievements in the
conquest and occupation of the West, the South
was at last turned upon on every hand, rebuked,
proscribed, defeated. The history of the United
States, we have learned, was, from the settlement
at Jamestown to the surrender at Appomattox, a
long-drawn contest for mastery between New England and the South, — and the end of the contest
we know. All along the parallels of latitude ran

the rivalry, in those heroical days of toil and adventure during which population crossed the continent, like an army advancing its encampments. Up and down the great river of the continent, too, and beyond, up the slow incline of the vast steppes that lift themselves toward the crowning towers of the Rockies, — beyond that, again, in the gold-fields and upon the green plains of California, the race for ascendency struggled on, — till at length there was a final coming face to face, and the masterful folk who had come from the loins of New England won their consummate victory.

It is a very dramatic form for the story. One almost wishes it were true. How fine a unity it would give our epic ! But perhaps, after all, the real truth is more interesting. The life of the nation cannot be reduced to these so simple terms. These two great forces, of the North and of the South, unquestionably existed, — were unquestionably projected in their operation out upon the great plane of the continent, there to combine or repel, as circumstances might determine. But the people that went out from the North were not an unmixed people ; they came from the great Middle States as well as from New England. Their transplantation into the West was no more a reproduction of New England or New York or

Pennsylvania or New Jersey than Massachusetts was a reproduction of old England, or New Netherland a reproduction of Holland. The Southern people, too, whom they met by the western rivers and upon the open prairies, were transformed, as they themselves were, by the rough fortunes of the frontier. A mixture of peoples, a modification of mind and habit, a new round of experiment and adjustment amidst the novel life of the baked and untilled plain, and the far valleys with the virgin forests still thick upon them: a new temper, a new spirit of adventure, a new impatience of restraint, a new license of life, — these are the characteristic notes and measures of the time when the nation spread itself at large upon the continent, and was transformed from a group of colonies into a family of States.

The passes of these eastern mountains were the arteries of the nation's life. The real breath of our growth and manhood came into our nostrils when first, like Governor Spotswood and that gallant company of Virginian gentlemen that rode with him in the far year 1716, the Knights of the Order of the Golden Horseshoe, our pioneers stood upon the ridges of the eastern hills and looked down upon those reaches of the continent where lay the untrodden paths of the westward migration.

There, upon the courses of the distant rivers that gleamed before them in the sun, down the farther slopes of the hills beyond, out upon the broad fields that lay upon the fertile banks of the " Father of Waters," up the long tilt of the continent to the vast hills that looked out upon the Pacific — there were the regions in which, joining with people from every race and clime under the sun, they were to make the great compounded nation whose liberty and mighty works of peace were to cause all the world to stand at gaze. Thither were to come Frenchmen, Scandinavians, Celts, Dutch, Slavs, — men of the Latin races and of the races of the Orient, as well as men, a great host, of the first stock of the settlements: English, Scots, Scots-Irish, — like New England men, but touched with the salt of humor, hard, and yet neighborly too. For this great process of growth by grafting, of modification no less than of expansion, the colonies, — the original thirteen States, — were only pre-liminary studies and first experiments. But the experiments that most resembled the great methods by which we peopled the continent from side to side and knit a single polity across all its length and breadth, were surely the experiments made from the very first in the Middle States of our Atlantic seaboard.

Here from the first were mixture of population, variety of element, combination of type, as if of the nation itself in small. Here was never a simple body, a people of but a single blood and extraction, a polity and a practice brought straight from one motherland. The life of these States was from the beginning like the life of the country: they have always shown the national pattern. In New England and the South it was very different. There some of the great elements of the national life were long in preparation: but separately and with an individual distinction ; without mixture, — for long almost without movement. That the elements thus separately prepared were of the greatest importance, and run everywhere like chief threads of the pattern through all our subsequent life, who can doubt? They give color and tone to every part of the figure. The very fact that they are so distinct and separately evident throughout, the very emphasis of individuality they carry with them, but proves their distinct origin. The other elements of our life, various though they be, and of the very fibre, giving toughness and consistency to the fabric, are merged in its texture, united, confused, almost indistinguishable, so thoroughly are they mixed, intertwined, interwoven, like the essential strands of the stuff itself: but these of the Puritan and the Southerner, though they run everywhere with the rest and seem upon a superficial view themselves the body of the cloth, in fact modify rather than make it.

What in fact has been the course of American history? How is it to be distinguished from European history? What features has it of its own, which give it its distinctive plan and movement? We have suffered, it is to be feared, a very serious limitation of view until recent years by having all our history written in the East. It has smacked strongly of a local flavor. It has concerned itself too exclusively with the origins and Old-World derivations of our story. Our historians have made their march from the sea with their heads over shoulder, their gaze always backward upon the landing-places and homes of the first settlers. In spite of the steady immigration, with its persistent tide of foreign blood, they have chosen to speak often and to think always of our people as sprung after all from a common stock, bearing a family likeness in every branch, and following all the while old, familiar, family ways. The view is the more misleading because it is so large a part of the truth without being all of it. The common British stock did first make the country, and has always set the pace. There were common institutions up and down the coast ; and these had formed and hardened for a persistent growth before the great westward migration began which was to re-shape and modify every element of our life. The national government itself was set up and made strong by success while yet we lingered for the most part upon the eastern coast and feared a too distant frontier.

But, the beginnings once safely made, change set in apace. Not only so : there had been slow change from the first. We have no frontier now, we are told, — except a broken fragment, it may be, here and there in some barren corner of the western lands, where some inhospitable mountain still shoulders us out, or where men are still lacking to break the baked surface of the plains and occupy them in the very teeth of hostile nature. But at first it was all frontier, — a mere strip of settlements stretched precariously upon the sea-edge of the wilds : an untouched continent in front of them, and behind them an unfrequented sea that almost never showed so much as the momentary gleam of a sail. Every step in the slow process of settlement was but a step of the same kind as the first, an advance to a new frontier like the old. For long we lacked, it is true, that new breed of frontiersmen born in after years beyond the mountains. Those first frontiersmen had still a touch of the timidity of the Old World in their blood: they lacked the frontier heart. They were " Pilgrims " in very fact, — exiled, not at home. Fine courage they had: and a steadfastness in their bold design which it does a faint-hearted age good to look back upon. There was no thought of drawing back. Steadily, almost calmly, they extended their seats. They built homes, and deemed it certain their children would live there after them. But they did not love the rough, uneasy life for its own sake. How long did they keep, if they could, within sight of the sea! The wilderness was their refuge; but how long before it became their joy and hope! Here was their destiny cast; but their hearts lingered and held back. It was only as generations passed and the work widened about them that their thought also changed, and a new thrill sped along their blood. Their life had been new and strange from their first landing in the wilderness. Their houses, their food, their clothing, their neighborhood dealings were all such as only the frontier brings. Insensibly they were themselves changed. The strange life became familiar; their adjustment to it was at length unconscious and without effort; they had no plans which were not inseparably a part and a product of it. But, until they had turned their backs once for all upon the sea; until they saw their western borders cleared of the French; until the mountain passes had grown familiar, and the lands beyond the central and constant theme of their hope, the goal and dream of their young men, they did not become an American people.

When they did, the great determining movement of our history began. The very visages of the people changed. That alert movement of the eye, that openness to every thought of enterprise or adventure, that nomadic habit which knows no fixed home and has plans ready to be carried any whither, —all the marks of the authentic type of the " American " as we know him came into our life. The crack of the whip and the song of the teamster, the heaving chorus of boatmen poling their heavy rafts upon the rivers, the laughter of the camp, the sound of bodies of men in the still forests, became the characteristic notes in our air. A roughened race, embrowned in the sun, hardened in manner by a coarse life of change and danger, loving the rude woods and the crack of the rifle, living to begin something new every day, striking with the broad and open hand, delicate in nothing but the touch of the trigger, leaving cities in its track as if by accident rather than design, settling again to the steady ways of a fixed life only when

it must : such was the American people whose
achievement it was to be to take possession of their
continent from end to end ere their national government was a single century old.   The picture is a
very singular one !   Settled life and wild side by
side : civilization frayed at the edges, — taken forward in rough and ready fashion, with a song and
a swagger, — not by statesmen, but by woodsmen
and drovers, with axes and whips and rifles in their
hands, clad in buckskin, like huntsmen.

It has been said that we have here repeated
some of the first processes of history ; that the
life and methods of our frontiersmen take us back
to the fortunes and hopes of the men who crossed
Europe when her forests, too, were still thick upon
her.   But the difference is really very fundamental,
and much more worthy of remark than the likeness.   Those shadowy masses of men whom we see
moving upon the face of the earth in the far-
away, questionable days when states were forming :
even those stalwart figures we see so well as they
emerge from the deep forests of Germany, to dis-
place the Roman in all his western provinces and
set up the states we know and marvel upon at this
day, show us men working their new work at their
own level.   They do not turn back a long cycle of
years from the old and settled states, the ordered

cities, the tilled fields, and the elaborated governments of an ancient civilization, to begin as it were
once more at the beginning. They carry alike
their homes and their states with them in the camp
and upon the ordered march of the host. They
are men of the forest, or else men hardened always
to take the sea in open boats. They live no more
roughly in the new lands than in the old. The
world has been frontier for them from the first.
They may go forward with their life in these new
seats from where they left off in the old. How
different the circumstances of our first settlement
and the building of new states on this side the
sea! Englishmen, bred in law and ordered government ever since the Norman lawyers were followed
a long five hundred years ago across the narrow
seas by those masterful administrators of the strong
Plantagenet race, leave an ancient realm and come
into a wilderness where states have never been ;
leave a land of art and letters, which saw but yes-
terday " the spacious times of great Elizabeth,"
where Shakespeare still lives in the gracious leisure
of his closing days at Stratford, where cities teem
with trade and men go bravely dight in cloth of
gold, and turn back six centuries, — nay, a thousand
years and more, — to the first work of building
states in a wilderness! They bring the steadied

habits and sobered thoughts of an ancient realm into the wild air of an untouched continent. The weary stretches of a vast sea lie, like a full thousand years of time, between them and the life in which till now all their thought was bred. Here they stand, as it were, with all their tools left behind, centuries struck out of their reckoning, driven back upon the long dormant instincts and forgotten craft of their race, not used this long age. Look how singular a thing: the work of a primitive race, the thought of a civilized! Hence the strange, almost grotesque groupings of thought and affairs in that first day of our history. Subtle politicians speak the phrases and practice the arts of intricate diplomacy from council chambers placed within log huts within a clearing. Men in ruffs and lace and polished shoe-buckles thread the lonely glades of primeval forests. The microscopical distinctions of the schools, the thin notes of a metaphysical theology are woven in and out through the labyrinths of grave sermons that run hours long upon the still air of the wilderness. Belief in dim refinements of dogma is made the test for man or woman who seeks admission to a company of pioneers. When went there by an age since the great flood when so singular a thing was seen as this: thousands of civilized men suddenly rusticated and bade do the work of primitive peoples, — Europe *frontiered !*

Of course there was a deep change wrought, if not in these men, at any rate in their children; and every generation saw the change deepen. It must seem to every thoughtful man a notable thing how, while the change was wrought, the simples of things complex were revealed in the clear air of the New World: how all accidentals seemed to fall away from the structure of government, and the simple first principles were laid bare that abide always; how social distinctions were stripped off, shown to be the mere cloaks and masks they were, and every man brought once again to a clear realization of his actual relations to his fellows! It was as if trained and sophisticated men had been rid of a sudden of their sophistication and of all the theory of their life, and left with nothing but their discipline of faculty, a schooled and sobered instinct. And the fact that we kept always, for close upon three hundred years, a like element in our life, a frontier people always in our van, is, so far, the central and determining fact of our national history. " East " and " West," an ever-changing line, but an unvarying experience and a constant leaven of change working always within the body of our folk. Our political, our economic, our social life has felt this potent influence from the wild border all our history through. The "West" is the great word of our history. The "Westerner" has been the type and master of our American life. Now at length, as I have said, we have lost our frontier: our front lies almost unbroken along all the great coast line of the western sea. The Westerner, in some day soon to come, will pass out of our life, as he so long ago passed out of the life of the Old World. Then a new epoch will open for us. Perhaps it has opened already. Slowly we shall grow old, compact our people, study the delicate adjustments of an intricate society, and ponder the niceties, as we have hitherto pondered the bulks and structural framework, of government. Have we not, indeed, already come to these things? But the past we know. We can "see it steady and see it whole;" and its central movement and motive are gross and obvious to the eye.

Till the first century of the Constitution is rounded out we stand all the while in the presence of that stupendous westward movement which has filled the continent: so vast, so various, at times so tragical, so swept by passion. Through all the long time there has been a line of rude settlements along our front wherein the same tests of power and of institutions were still being made that were made first upon the sloping banks of the rivers of old Virginia and within the long sweep of the Bay of Massachusetts. The new life of the West has reacted all the while — who shall say how powerfully? — upon the older life of the East; and yet the East has moulded the West as if she sent forward to it through every decade of the long process the chosen impulses and suggestions of history. The West has taken strength, thought, training, selected aptitudes out of the old treasures of the East, — as if out of a new Orient; while the East has itself been kept fresh, vital, alert, originative by the West, her blood quickened all the while, her youth through every age renewed. Who can say in a word, in a sentence, in a volume, what destinies have been variously wrought, with what new examples of growth and energy, while, upon this unexampled scale, community has passed beyond community across the vast reaches of this great continent!

The great process is the more significant because it has been distinctively a national process. Until the Union was formed and we had consciously set out upon a separate national career, we moved but timidly across the nearer hills. Our most remote settlements lay upon the rivers and in the open glades of Tennessee and Kentucky. It was in the years that immediately succeeded the war of 1812 that the movement into the West began to be a mighty migration. Till then our eyes had been more often in the East than in the West. Not only were foreign questions to be settled and our standing among the nations to be made good, but we still remained acutely conscious and deliberately conservative of our Old-World connections. For all we were so new a people and lived so simple and separate a life, we had still the sobriety and the circumspect fashions of action that belong to an old society. We were, in government and manners, but a disconnected part of the world beyond the seas. Its thought and habit still set us our standards of speech and action. And this, not because of imitation, but because of actual and long abiding political and social connection with the mother country. Our statesmen, — strike but the names of Samuel Adams and Patrick Henry from the list, together with all like untutored spirits, who stood for the new, unreverencing ardor of a young democracy, — our statesmen were such men as might have taken their places in the House of Commons or in the Cabinet at home as naturally and with as easy an adjustment to their place and task as in the Continental Congress or in the immortal Constitutional Convention. Think of the stately ways and the grand air and the authoritative social understandings of the generation that set the new government afoot, — the generation of Washington and John Adams. Think, too, of the conservative tradition that guided all the early history of that government: that early line of gentlemen Presidents: that steady " cabinet succession to the Presidency " which came at length to seem almost like an oligarchy to the impatient men who were shut out from it. The line ended, with a sort of chill, in stiff John Quincy Adams, too cold a man to be a people's prince after the old order of Presidents; and the year 1829, which saw Jackson come in, saw the old order go out.

The date is significant. Since the war of 1812, undertaken as if to set us free to move westward, seven States had been admitted to the Union: and the whole number of States was advanced to twenty-four. Eleven new States had come into partnership with the old thirteen. The voice of the West rang through all our counsels; and, in Jackson, the new partners took possession of the Government. It is worth while to remember how men stood amazed at the change: how startled, chagrined, dismayed the conservative States of the East were at the revolution they saw effected, the riot of change they saw set in; and no man who

has once read the singular story can forget how
the eight years Jackson reigned saw the Government, and politics themselves, transformed. For
long, — the story being written in the regions
where the shock and surprise of the change was
greatest, — the period of this momentous revolution was spoken of amongst us as a period of
degeneration, the birth-time of a deep and permanent demoralization in our politics. But we see it
differently now. Whether we have any taste or
stomach for that rough age or not, however much
we may wish that the old order might have stood,
the generation of Madison and Adams have been
prolonged, and the good tradition of the early days
handed on unbroken and unsullied, we now know
that what the nation underwent in that day of
change was not degeneration, great and perilous as
were the errors of the time, but regeneration.
The old order was changed, once and for all. A
new nation stepped, with a touch of swagger, upon
the stage, — a nation which had broken alike with
the traditions and with the wisely wrought experience of the Old World, and which, with all the
haste and rashness of youth, was minded to work
out a separate policy and destiny of its own. It
was a day of hazards, but there was nothing sinister
at the heart of the new plan. It was a wasteful

experiment, to fling out, without wise guides, upon untried ways; but an abounding continent afforded enough and to spare even for the wasteful. It was sure to be so with a nation that came out of the secluded vales of a virgin continent. It was the bold frontier voice of the West sounding in affairs. The timid shivered, but the robust waxed strong and rejoiced, in the tonic air of the new day.

It was then we swung out into the main paths of our history. The new voices that called us were first silvery, like the voice of Henry Clay, and spoke old familiar words of eloquence. The first spokesmen of the West even tried to con the classics, and spoke incongruously in the phrases of politics long dead and gone to dust, as Benton did. But presently the tone changed, and it was the truculent and masterful accents of the real frontiersman that rang dominant above the rest, harsh, impatient, and with an evident dash of temper. The East slowly accustomed itself to the change; caught the movement, though it grumbled and even trembled at the pace; and managed most of the time to keep in the running. But it was always henceforth to be the West that set the pace. There is no mistaking the questions that have ruled our spirits as a nation during the present century. The public land question, the tariff question, and the question of slavery, — these dominate from first to last. It was the West that made each one of these the question that it was. Without the free lands to which every man who chose might go, there would not have been that easy prosperity of life and that high standard of abundance which seemed to render it necessary that, if we were to have manufactures and a diversified industry at all, we should foster new undertakings by a system of protection which would make the profits of the factory as certain and as abundant as the profits of the farm. It was the constant movement of the population, the constant march of wagon trains into the West, that made it so cardinal a matter of policy whether the great national domain should *be* free land or not: and that was the land question. It was the settlement of the West that transformed slavery from an accepted institution into passionate matter of controversy.

Slavery within the States of the Union stood sufficiently protected by every solemn sanction the Constitution could afford. No man could touch it there, think, or hope, or purpose what he might. But where new States were to be made it was not so. There at every step choice must be made: slavery or no slavery? — a new choice for every new State: a fresh act of origination to go with every fresh act of organization. Had there been no Territories, there could have been no slavery question, except by revolution and contempt of fundamental law. But with a continent to be peopled, the choice thrust itself insistently forward at every step and upon every hand. This was the slavery question : not what should be done to reverse the past, but what should be done to redeem the future. It was so men of that day saw it, — and so also must historians see it. We must not mistake the programme of the Anti-Slavery Society for the platform of the Republican party, or forget that the very war itself was begun ere any purpose of abolition took shape amongst those who were statesmen and in authority. It was a question, not of freeing men, but of preserving a Free Soil. Kansas showed us what the problem was, not South Carolina : and it was the Supreme Court, not the slave-owners, who formulated the matter for our thought and purpose.

And so, upon every hand and throughout every national question, was the commerce between East and West made up: that commerce and exchange of ideas, inclinations, purposes, and principles which has constituted the moving force of our life as a nation. Men illustrate the operation of these singular forces better than questions can : and no man illustrates it better than Abraham Lincoln.

> "Great captains with their guns and drums
>   Disturb our judgment for the hour;
>   But at last silence comes :
>   These all are gone, and, standing like a tower,
>   Our children shall behold his fame,
>   The kindly-earnest, brave, foreseeing man,
>   Sagacious, patient, dreading praise not blame,
>   New birth of our new soil, the first American."

It is a poet's verdict; but it rings in the authentic tone of the seer. It must be also the verdict of history. He would be a rash man who should say he understood Abraham Lincoln. No doubt natures deep as his, and various almost to the point of self-contradiction, can be sounded only by the judgment of men of a like sort, — if any such there be. But some things we all may see and judge concerning him. You have in him the type and flower of our growth. It is as if Nature had made a typical American, and then had added with liberal hand the royal quality of genius, to show us what the type could be. Lincoln owed nothing to his birth, everything to his growth: had no training save what he gave himself; no nurture, but only a wild and native strength. His life was his schooling, and every day of it gave to his character a new touch of development. His manhood not only, but his perception also, expanded with his life. His eyes, as they looked more and more abroad, beheld the national life, and comprehended it : and the lad who had been so rough-cut a provincial became, when grown to manhood, the one leader in all the nation who held the whole people singly in his heart : — held even the Southern people there, and would have won them back. And so we have in him what we must call the perfect development of native strength, the rounding out and nationalization of the provincial. Andrew Jackson was a type, not of the nation, but of the West. For all the tenderness there was in the stormy heart of the masterful man, and staunch and simple loyalty to all who loved him, he learned nothing in the East; kept always the flavor of the rough school in which he had been bred ; was never more than a frontier soldier and gentleman. Lincoln differed from Jackson by all the length of his unmatched capacity to learn. Jackson could understand only men of his own kind; Lincoln could understand men of all sorts and from every region of the land : seemed himself, indeed, to be all men by turns, as mood succeeded mood in his strange nature. He never ceased to stand, in his bony angles, the express image of the ungainly frontiersman. His mind never lost the vein of coarseness that had marked him grossly when a youth. And yet how he grew and strengthened in the real stuff of dignity and greatness: how nobly he could bear himself without the aid of grace! He kept always the shrewd and seeing eye of the woodsman and the hunter, and the flavor of wild life never left him : and yet how easily his view widened to great affairs ; how surely he perceived the value and the significance of whatever touched him and made him neighbor to itself !

Lincoln's marvelous capacity to extend his comprehension to the measure of what he had in hand is the one distinguishing mark of the man : and to study the development of that capacity in him is little less than to study, where it is as it were perfectly registered, the national life itself. This boy lived his youth in Illinois when it was a frontier State. The youth of the State was coincident with his own : and man and State kept equal pace in their striding advance to maturity. The frontier population was an intensely political population. It felt to the quick the throb of the nation's life, — for the nation's life ran through it, going its eager way to the westward. The West was not separate from the East. Its communities were every day receiving fresh members from the East, and the fresh impulse of direct suggestion. Their

blood flowed to them straight from the warmest
veins of the older communities. More than that,
elements which were separated in the East were
mingled in the West: which displayed to the eye
as it were a sort of epitome of the most active and
permanent forces of the national life. In such
communities as these Lincoln mixed daily from the
first with men of every sort and from every quarter
of the country. With them he discussed neighborhood politics, the politics of the State, the politics
of the nation, — and his mind became traveled as
he talked. How plainly amongst such neighbors,
there in Illinois, must it have become evident that
national questions were centring more and more in
the West as the years went by: coming as it were
to meet them. Lincoln went twice down the
Mississippi, upon the slow rafts that carried wares
to its mouth, and saw with his own eyes, so used
to look directly and point-blank upon men and
affairs, characteristic regions of the South. He
worked his way slowly and sagaciously, with that
larger sort of sagacity which so marked him all his
life, into the active business of state politics; sat
twice in the state legislature, and then for a term
in Congress, — his sensitive and seeing mind open
all the while to every turn of fortune and every
touch of nature in the moving affairs he looked

upon. All the while, too, he continued to canvass, piece by piece, every item of politics, as of old, with his neighbors, familiarly around the stove, or upon the corners of the street, or more formally upon the stump; and kept always in direct contact with the ordinary views of ordinary men. Meanwhile he read, as nobody else around him read, and sought to gain a complete mastery over speech, with the conscious purpose to prevail in its use; derived zest from the curious study of mathematical proof, and amusement as well as strength from the practice of clean and naked statements of truth. It was all irregularly done, but strenuously, with the same instinct throughout, and with a steady access of facility and power. There was no sudden leap for this man, any more than for other men, from crudeness to finished power, from an understanding of the people of Illinois to an understanding of the people of the United States. And thus he came at last, with infinite pains and a wonder of endurance, to his great national task with a self-trained capacity which no man could match, and made upon a scale as liberal as the life of the people. You could not then set this athlete a pace in learning or in perceiving that was too hard for him. He knew the people and their life as no other man did or could: and now stands in his place singular in all the annals of mankind, the " brave, sagacious, foreseeing, patient man " of the people, " new birth of our new soil, the first American."

We have here a national man presiding over sectional men. Lincoln understood the East better than the East understood him or the people from whom he sprung : and this is every way a very noteworthy circumstance. For my part, I read a lesson in the singular career of this great man. Is it possible the East remains sectional while the West broadens to a wider view ?

" Be strong-backed, brown-handed, upright as your pines ;
   By the scale of a hemisphere shape your designs,"

is an inspiring programme for the woodsman and the pioneer ; but how are you to be brown-handed in a city office ? What if you never see the upright pines ? How are you to have so big a purpose on so small a part of the hemisphere ? As it has grown old, unquestionably, the East has grown sectional. There is no suggestion of the prairie in its city streets, or of the embrowned ranchman and farmer in its well-dressed men. Its ports teem with shipping from Europe and the Indies. Its newspapers run upon the themes of an Old World. It hears of the great plains of the continent as of foreign parts, which it may never think to see except from a car window. Its life is self-centred and selfish. The West, save where special interests centre (as in those pockets of silver where men's eyes catch as it were an eager gleam from the very ore itself) : the West is in less danger of sectionalization. Who shall say in that wide country where one region ends and another begins, or, in that free and changing society, where one class ends and another begins?

This, surely, is the moral of our history. The East has spent and been spent for the West : has given forth her energy, her young men and her substance, for the new regions that have been a-making all the century through. But has she learned as much as she has taught, or taken as much as she has given? Look what it is that has now at last taken place. The westward march has stopped, upon the final slopes of the Pacific ; and now the plot thickens. Populations turn upon their old paths ; fill in the spaces they passed by neglected in their first journey in search of a land of promise ; settle to a life such as the East knows as well as the West, — nay, much better. With the change, the pause, the settlement, our people draw into closer groups, stand face to face, to know each other and be known : and the time has come for the East to learn in her turn ; to broaden her understanding of political and economic conditions to the scale of a hemisphere, as her own poet bade. Let us be sure that we get the national temperament; send our minds abroad upon the continent, become neighbors to all the people that live upon it, and lovers of them all, as Lincoln was.

Read but your history aright, and you shall not find the task too hard. Your own local history, look but deep enough, tells the tale you must take to heart. Here upon our own seaboard, as truly as ever in the West, was once a national frontier, with an elder East beyond the seas. Here, too, various peoples combined, and elements separated elsewhere effected a tolerant and wholesome mixture. Here, too, the national stream flowed full and strong, bearing a thousand things upon its currents. Let us resume and keep the vision of that time; know ourselves, our neighbors, our destiny, with lifted and open eyes; see our history truly, in its great proportions; be ourselves liberal as the great principles we profess; and so be the people who might have again the heroic adventures and do again the heroic work of the past. 'T is thus we shall renew our youth and secure our age against decay.

www.ingramcontent.com/pod-product-compliance
Lightning Source LLC
Chambersburg PA
CBHW020058030726
47498CB00006B/1847